Doctor Mark Solace

The Lazarus Seed

-

By Stephen Critchlow

Edited by Phoebe Critchlow
Book cover designed by Ru Gupte

Foreword

This novella is entirely the work of my late father Stephen Critchlow (or Critch as he was known by everyone but his parents). In the time I knew him he was a father, comrade and friend to me. He was an incredibly funny man who had a terrible habit of causing laughter to break out in any room he entered. He was an actor by profession delighting in performing stories across; film, television stage and radio.

He was also a big reader and would swallow up horror anthology books from classic's like the works of Lovecraft, Poe to Arthur C. Clark. The passion he had for these stories about the strange and absurd lead him to creating Doctor Solace. A pet project of his for some time. The Lazarus Seed was the only novel he wrote. He was very enthusiastic about getting this story produced and to have people read and enjoy it. He spent many months at the computer typing this out on a free version of Word Excel with two fingers. After he passed I wanted to make sure that his wish to have Doctor Solace out there came true.

He was always passionate about the supernatural and his enjoyment of Sherlock Holmes and otherworldly 70s shows are clear in The Lazarus Seed.

Doctor Lazarus is a reflection of my father in some respects; it's clear that he borrowed elements from his own life. Sir Barnard Spilsbury his faithful St Bernard was based on our gentle family labrador Milo. The Eagle was a pub he found whilst on tour and enjoyed thoroughly. The oddest part for me whilst going through this was the fact that Solace's wife

Caroline died and Solace struggles with his grief. My father named her after his wife (my mother) Caroline Lawrie. In some bizarre way my dad was working out how he would feel if she'd died. Which is very odd to read when he was the one she was grieving for.

I enjoyed editing and recording the audiobook for this story as I think it is a fun adventure tale with exciting twists and turns. I hope anyone who loves 60s/70s Pulp fiction finds this book as I think it would appeal strongly to them too.

By Phoebe Critchlow

Jesus said to her; "Your brother will rise again." John 11.23

Prologue:

An Extract from the Journal of Richard Carter -

The Belgian Congo (May 1936).

The Congo River Basin covers almost 1,000,000 square kilometres. This vast plateau shaped area is covered by a tropical rain forest and criss-crossed by rivers. The centre is surrounded by mountainous terraces in the west and plateaus merging into savannahs in the south and southwest.

This dry, literal description goes little way to capture the sheer scale and other worldliness of the place I have found myself working and studying these last two months. The climate is hot and humid here and the rainy season can last from October to May. Violent thunderstorms descend without warning, pummeling our encampment and making our work arduous. After which, an all-engulfing steam rises giving way to a vision of the most incredible array of flora and fauna the human eye has ever witnessed.

Before entering my final year at Cambridge, and with my eye firmly on a place at The Institute of Tropical Medicine, myself and two others enrolled on what was then rather pompously named a "Civilizing

Mission". In short, a European incentive to turn a "primitive society" into the western capitalist model. This wasn't our ambition. We simply wanted to go over there and see for ourselves. To experience a totally different culture. To use our skills, gain knowledge and perhaps help. And yes, take something of that knowledge back with us. This wasn't an altruistic mission by any stretch of the imagination. We wanted to come back home with something to show for our efforts. That sharp, hard ambition that young men have to leave their stamp on the world.

We had joined a small but well-established mission some twelve miles north of Kahuzi-Biega. Over the ensuing weeks myself and my colleagues were put to good use by a sullen British clergyman called Baxter and his aide, a friendly local man named Amba. We used our burgeoning skills to help the small but steady flow of sick and injured natives that made the not insignificant trek through the forest to our huts by the side of the river. Any spare time was devoted to studying the multitudinous plant life that sprang up around us. Analysing them and trying to document any as yet unknown species.

My knowledge of medicine was limited compared with that of my colleagues but we helped each other as our friendships grew and in a relatively short space of time I found I could treat the majority of the patients that entered our camp even if success was of a marginal nature. Our medical facilities were severely limited and our medicines in short supply in the war against such endemic diseases as malaria, yellow fever and the horror of cholera due to the natives' limited access to clean water. The days were long and taxing but we felt energised with a purpose we had never experienced in the cosseted halls and laboratories of Cambridge University.

It was the afternoon of the 12th of April when a man walked out of the forest into our encampment. He was carrying a small boy in his arms. I could see from fifty yards away that the boy was in the last throes of Malaria. He was totally emaciated with a thin film of sweat covering his face. My colleagues were on a fact-finding mission. Gathering samples near The Ruwenzori Range. I held out little hope for the boy, whose breathing was extremely shallow and I guessed was around six years old. The father, as I assumed him to be, was beside himself with despair. I tried to comfort him and with what little Congolese I had learned assured him I would do my best and that God would do the rest. He was to leave him in my care and I would do all I could to nurse him back to health. The words felt hollow on my lips and I knew I would be digging another small grave at the back of our makeshift hospital in a short space of time. He left somewhat reassured by my performance and I carried the frail bag of bones in my charge up the wooden steps and into what passed for my surgery.

Four doses of quinine followed by mefloquine did nothing to allay the clotting that had taken place and I didn't have the equipment for a blood transfusion. There was nothing I could do but watch him die. He was by no means the first I had seen pass beyond but he was certainly the youngest. He wouldn't have reached me without the determination of his father and I failed to save him. I made a note of the time. All signs of life stopped at 3.37pm. I covered his head, walked out onto the porch, sat down and wept. I think it must have been due to the boy's age coupled with fatigue.

Sometime later, as the forest light was thickening into evening, I had a large glass of Scotch and resigned myself to dig a small grave for the child I had failed to save. One of at least twenty similar mounds that hid behind our ill-equipped missionary hospital on the banks of the Lualaba River. I stepped out of my hut and noticed a figure standing at about roughly the same place as the father had stood earlier. I was suddenly struck with an apprehension that he had come back and I was faced with explaining to the bereaved parent his worst nightmares had come into being. Then as my vision improved, I realised that this figure wasn't who I imagined it to be.

An incredibly tall man was standing watching me. Stick thin and wearing a goat skin loincloth. There was something about his stance and tilt of his head that unnerved me. It was as if he were too still. It was inexplicable but I felt my mouth go dry and cold sweat spring up on my forehead. As I mentioned, he was roughly fifty yards away but I somehow felt he was next to me and this caused in me a disorientation rather like being at sea. He moved across the distance between us. Covering the ground quickly and with a cat-like smoothness. He passed me without speaking and entered the hut where the dead boy was still laying. I followed, vainly gathering my thoughts and nerve. The man must have been close to seven feet tall with startling ice blue eyes. That looked through me rather than at me. I asked him what he wanted here and what I could do to help. He didn't reply but instead lifted the sheet that covered the boy's body and looked at the corpse below.

I explained in a stammering fashion the events leading up to the poor child's demise. That I had done my best and it was all I could have done with the limited means at my disposal. By then I had assumed that the giant was a relative or head man of a nearby village and had come to see if anything could be done to save the boy. In which case there was every chance that I was pleading for my life. He seemed not to take any notice as he moved the child's head from side to side gently yet oddly with an air of professionalism, as if he were some form of exotic physician and the child were his patient.

He lifted the child's head and placed

his massive hand on the nape of his neck, from what I could see around The Atlas that connects the skull to the spine. At that point he closed his eyes and I swear said something under his breath in a low metallic growl which I didn't recognise to be Congolese. Then he turned his gaze on me. The air seemed to freeze around us as if one species looked upon another for the first time. I do not know for how long I stood there transfixed. Later I was convinced that at that precise moment that man could have picked me up and carried me off and I would have been powerless to move a muscle. Instead, he reached into the folds of his loin cloth and then held out a shovel sized hand.

Opening his palm, he revealed a quantity of small seeds roughly the size of watermelon pips but of a shiny gunmetal grey. He picked one out and mimed putting it into his mouth then pointed at the boy's mouth.

I reiterated that the boy had sadly passed away a good two hours ago. That his journey was futile. He slowly shook his head as if he could understand me and repeated the mime. He then opened the child's mouth and put the seed inside and tenderly closed it again. He then put the other seeds in my hand. His hand dwarfing mine like a parent would an infant and a warm, not unpleasant feeling passed through me. Followed by a slight dizziness. Oddly I don't recall the texture of his hand. Just a vibration. Then he left the hut. His head dipping low under the door frame and the forest swallowed him up. Like he had never been. I stood at the head of the child's bed and after a minute started to shake with relief.

I know the child died that day. The 12th of April at 3.37pm. I know his heart stopped and all his organs ceased to function. I know there was no pulse and all his breath had left his body. Yet two hours after that man left my hut, the boy sat up.

Chapter 1
*Imperial Caesar Dead and Turned To clay -
Hamlet Act 5 Scene 2*

22nd Of July 1966

The party was winding down. The last pockets of resistance were finishing their conversations and drinks. Beaten by the old enemy, the clock on the wall. Which, at this point in the proceedings, churlishly reminded them it that was almost half past two in the morning. Coats were being got and cabs sorted. Numbers were being exchanged and promises of further social gatherings made, before the last stragglers stumbled bleary eyed out onto the wet South Kensington streets. It had been an interesting evening. Not because of the guests thought Doctor Mark Solace, rubbing his itchy, tired eyes and finishing the last of his Malbec. The guests had made up the usual collection of Cambridge University types. Cynical, dry, work based conversations had turned into false bonhomie as the drink took effect. He had longed for the odd joke or slightly racy story. In fact, it was only a minor classics lecturer, Smollets recipe for Chilli Con Carne, that involved dropping a live Mars Bar into the mix that had stuck in his memory. He wondered, given his coordination skills, if Smollets discovery was more luck than judgment.

Normally university Professors did not give parties like this. They might have a perfunctory pint at The Wheatsheaf with one or two fellow academics. Talk a bit of shop, grumble about funding and head off home. The reason why tonight's gathering was interesting to Solace were the hosts. Doctor Richard Carter and his wife Diana were, in his limited experience, reserved and bookish people. One would perhaps somewhat harshly describe Doctor Carter as a bit "near" with his money to use a Yorkshire term. Solace had only socially drunk with him once at a college Christmas party. He recalled Carter having a glass of dry sherry and vanishing before the Carols started and the charity tin passed. His wife Diana, he gleaned, was a shy yet kind woman who organised fundraising events for the campus but very much in the background. He had bumped into her once by accident as he turned the corner of the quad at Hughes Hall. She had made a gabled apology, although it was his fault, avoiding eye contact, before dashing off. So why, thought Solace averting his eyes from the kitchen clock yet again, were they suddenly both behaving like Richard Burton and Elizabeth Taylor. Apparently, they had recently returned from a skiing trip to Bern, another out of character choice mused Solace, where Mrs Carter had suffered a terrible fall.

Cracking her skull and having to be airlifted off the Piste. He had heard it was touch and go but thanks to the ministrations of a friend who was one of their party she had made a full recovery.

She certainly had that alright thought Solace, as Mrs Carter's laugh peeled out again as it had done all evening with no sign of abating. He glanced over into the living room where she sat. He could only see the back of her head. Chestnut brown hair recently cut into a bob, she was leaning forward whispering into the ear of Professor Leung, head of Mandarin, with her hand resting lazily on his knee. His face a mixture of bemusement and acute embarrassment. Well, thought Solace, perhaps this was what near death experiences do for people. Why not? You've only got one life and all the rest of the usual vacuous sayings that people spout. He was trying to think of some more, stalling the moment he had to leave, when a young voice above him said "One for the stairs Doctor Solace?" He looked up and saw the Carter's daughter Josephine standing there. She had been playing the part of unpaid waitress and washer upper all evening. Enthusiastically moving amongst the thirsty of the camp like Henry the Fifth on the eve of Agincourt. A little touch of Jo in the night thought Solace. Then checked himself. "Dive thoughts down to my soul". Drink always made him think in Shakespeare quotations and get leary. Ah, he replied, "The middle-class alternative to "Last Orders at the bar ladies and Gents!" immediately regretting his impromptu cockney accent. "Thank you, no., I've picked up some fantastic recipes though which I intend to act upon when I get the chance." I'd leave out the Mars bar if I were you", smiled Jo. "Are you sure I can't twist your arm? "Better not" returned Solace "I've got an elderly friend that needs my attention". "Oh yes "she countered, "you could have brought Sir Bernard but I don't think he would have enjoyed the smoke and

noise. It's a shame though. I know daddy wanted to talk to you". "He would have had more joy with me than Sir Bernard" Solace said, getting to his feet. "But I'm sure we'll catch up soon."
Doubting that they would.

Suddenly Mrs Carter's Laugh rang out yet again and Solace marked the worry on her daughter's face. "Your Mums certainly the life and soul of the party tonight" he ventured, trying to raise the mood again. "That's not my mum," said Jo quietly. Silence. Solace felt all he could say in return to this bewildering statement was "I beg your pardon?" Just then Richard Carter hoved into view from the lounge where he'd been nervously overseeing events and half-heartedly taking part in conversations. "Oh, Mark! You're not going, are you? I've not had a chance to say hello" You've had four hours thought Solace but instead said "Sorry Richard. Lovely party and thanks very much for the invite but I've got an elderly friend at home that needs my attention. "Sir Bernard Spillsbury" Beamed Jo at her father. "Yes" said Solace "I've got to let him outside to do his business" Carter relaxed momentarily and smiled to let them know he was in on the joke. "It always makes me laugh Mark when I remember you had named your dog after arguably the greatest British pathologist of the twentieth century". It was the first time Jo had seen her father smile all night. "Well, it was either that or Leaky" replied Solace. "If you'll excuse me" cut in Jo "I think Professor Leung is making motions to go. Goodnight Dr Solace, see you again soon I hope."

"Can I get you a cab, Mark"? Asked Doctor Carter after Jo had gone and Solace noticed how tense and tired around the eyes he looked under the kitchen lights. "No", said Solace, "I'll get one on the street. Besides I need to walk off all that lovely food and wine you were generous enough to give me. And that's a lot of walking. My coat's the dark blue one by the mirror". As Doctor Carter Helped him on with his Trench coat Solace noticed that his hands were shaking almost violently." I say old man" said Solace with genuine concern in his voice "why don't you call it a night. You're dead on your feet". When Solace turned round. Carter was looking at him with what he took to be a mixture of accusation and fear. It was the look of a trapped animal and it shocked Solace to see it come from nowhere. "Why did you say that?" Carter's words came out as a sharp whisper." Well, er. Richard " said

Solace choosing his words carefully "these do's. You know, organised fun can be ruinous to one's health and I don't want your last sight on earth to be my ugly mug". He smiled disarmingly and Carter smiled back with a somewhat thinner variety. "Well", he said bitterly "When you've gotta go you've gotta go. As they say. It comes to us all in the end. At least...". He tailed off, lost in his thoughts. Things were getting dark again for poor old Carter and Solace decided to renege on his earlier self-promise concerning Shakespeare and reached for his trusty Complete works. Almost guaranteed to get him out of many a conversational cul-de-sac. Ah yes "imperial Caesar dead and turned to clay might stop a hole to keep the wind away". That got them to the front door. Opening it Carter smiled and extended a hand said "Goodnight Sweet prince". Solace returned the smile and a hand then remembered. "Oh do give my thanks to your wife" ...but the door closed with a slam and Carter was gone.

Solace let out a long heartfelt sigh of relief which turned into a yawn as the air changed temperature. He ambled down the three flights of stairs and out of the street door into the London morning. He paused for a moment, getting his bearings. After which, he crossed the street, nearly colliding with professor Leung as he shot past him without saying goodnight. While Solace stood for a while sobering up, gazing left and right for any sign of a passing cab, he glanced up and caught the light from the Carters window on the third floor and the figure framed there. The glow from a slowly passing bus shed some light on the shape only fleetingly, but Solace felt his breath catch in his throat and an icy hand grip the base of his spine which seemed to be pulling him down. At the same time, he felt his knees give and he sank slowly to the ground, trying to regulate his breathing and hold on to the wrought iron stair rail that was thankfully attached to the opposite building. He sat there shaking in a cold sweat, gazing at the curb. Two passing figures asked if he was alright... He simply nodded but kept his gaze downwards. Eventually, after a good few minutes his heart stopped pounding against his chest and his grip on the stair rail loosed. He carefully got to his feet before walking steadily off up Kensington High Street.

Chapter 2

Solace

Solace lay in bed missing his wife. The Sunday midday sun was streaming through a crack in his bedroom curtains. He felt the emptiness of his life without Caroline palpably like a punch to the gut. Today it was worse than it had been for a long time. She had been gone for a little over a year and he still thought of her every day. The pain coming over him in waves that gradually abated as he mastered it. Only to lay in wait before returning with renewed vigour. Triggered by anything that reminded him of her. He went through a phase where he thought he saw her everywhere. In a marketplace or library. Of course, it was impossible but still he would follow the unsuspecting victim until he could steal a look at their face. He'd had to stop that. The help from his friends and his work had kept him from giving up. Yet, he had poured over every argument they'd had like it was on loop. Unhealthy stuff Solace thought. Shaking his head in a gesture designed to rid himself of these thoughts he tried again to piece together the events of the previous night.

After he'd staggered to his feet

opposite the Carters flat he must have walked for over an hour until he felt calm enough to contemplate finding a cab. This he did and managed to stammer his address to the indifferent cabby. When he reached home the key in the lock woke Spillsbury and he heard his old Saint Bernard hobble up the hallway. "What do you mean? What time do you call this?" said Solace to his dog. (Solace had taken to inventing conversations with the animal that he found amusing and even comforting.) "Am I in the dog house?" He'd poured himself a stiff night cap and sat in his armchair working out as scientifically as possible what he had seen staring out of that third floor window. The face

had been that of Diana Carter. Without a doubt And yet it wasn't. He had only seen it briefly yet there was something carnal, even bestial about the features. There was a terrible feral quality that felt totally evil coming from the figure like beam of energy and reaching him with the power to knock him off his feet. And the eyes. There was something about the eyes. However, try as he may, every time Solace
tried to picture them, he couldn't. He shook involuntarily and tried to return his thoughts to some sort of normality.

This search for normality took Solace to The RAF Bar in The Eagle Tavern. The preferred watering hole of both British and American airmen who decorated the pub's ceiling with colourful and risqué pictures using candle wax and lipstick during their sojourn at air base Wyton in the dark days of World war Two. This comfortable, friendly pub was made famous in nineteen fifty-three when one cold February morning two young scientists, James Watson and Francis Crick, burst in and told the bemused clientele that they had discovered the structure of DNA. Solace smiled to himself as he pictured the sceptical glare of the young airman. He took another sip of his whiskey and glanced down at Spillsbury, fast asleep at his feet. The dog's left leg twitched as he chased rabbits in his dreams. He must have dozed off himself, the effects of his late night coupled with his second drink taking hold, when a short time later a brief, staccato cough brought him out of his revery.

A tall, balding, slightly overweight man in a long trench coat smiled down at him. He looked friendly enough but Solace sensed he was police. He had encountered enough of them over the years to know one when he saw one. "Doctor Mark

Solace?" enquired the man holding the smile and a steady gaze. Solace immediately felt guilty. He couldn't explain why, but he had that inbred, irrational worry that is shared by many when faced with an officer of the law. "Yes?" replied Solace shifting in his seat and pulling himself awake. "I'm Detective Inspector Wall" Solace noticed a slight London accent. The big man motioned to a seat across from Solace. "May I sit down sir?" Solace nodded quizzically. "But please be careful of my dog. He's catching up on his beauty sleep". The police man's smile widened and he carefully sat down admiring the old St Bernard at their feet. "He doesn't need much of that by the looks of things" smiled the policeman "He's a handsome old devil isn't he" Solace sensed it was up to him to move things forward. "What can I do for you Inspector?" DI Wall regarded him for a moment. He appeared to Solace either pensive or embarrassed. The room seemed to get darker, then the policeman cleared his throat "I understand you were at a party in London last night hosted by Professor Carter and his wife Diana. Would that be correct sir?" said Wall gravely. Solace focused his mind. "Yes, I was. Has something happened to them?" DI Wall leaned forward almost imperceptibly towards Solace and lowered his voice. Solace could detect the faint whiff of Brylcreem and

Palmolive soap. Plain, masculine aromas that fell in line with the image he saw before him. "I'm sorry to have to tell you this Doctor Solace" began Wall "but both Professor Carter and his wife were found dead at their home at around 9am this morning". Silence, thick and heavy, descended between the two men like a wall.

Time stopped briefly as the policeman gave Solace space to digest the information. Solace looked down at his drink, gaging his emotions. He admitted to himself privately that while this news was a shock, he didn't really feel a great deal. After all, they were only vague acquaintances. What he was starting to feel, however, was a growing sense of unease as to where all this was leading. "That's terrible" he said after a second searching for the right responses. "What on earth happened" DI Wall continued. "Their bodies were found by the cleaner when she arrived for her shift" Then he paused and Solace sensed that the Inspector had set sail from his comfort zone and was encountering choppy seas. Then he did something that he considered decidedly odd. "Doctor Solace" said Wall earnestly "could I buy you a drink, because I think I need one myself?" Solace requested a large Red Breast, an Irish Whiskey of particular note, the policeman rose and went to the bar leaving him in a state of bewilderment and more than a little anxious. Running through the previous evening in his mind and returning to that face at the window, Solace could find no clue to the events that might have happened after he left. Wall's departure had created a hiatus that was making Solace more than a little nervous. This was not normal police procedure. Had some atrocity happened at the Carters flat that meant he was implicated? He felt his mouth starting to go sticky.

Shortly Wall returned with their

drinks and sat down. "Sorry about that Doctor Solace" said Wall after Solace had thanked him "but I've had quite a morning and it doesn't look like getting any easier" "Please Inspector" said Solace feeling exasperation rise in his voice "For god's sake tell me what happened" Wall took a long drink of his pint. "Well," He began hesitantly "from what our forensics team can ascertain, Professor Carter was murdered by his wife who then suffered a brain seizure and died." It was Solace's turn to take a drink. He swore quietly under his breath. Then a thought struck him. "Have you told Josephine, their daughter, does she know?" "She was informed this morning" answered

Wall "A WPC is still with her as far as I know. She very kindly helped us try and piece together the events as best she could. Miss Carter says she did some tidying up after you and the rest of the guests left then left herself at about half past two." "Terrible". Muttered Solace not really knowing what to say or indeed why he was called upon to say it. Surely it wasn't the police's job to go around everyone who knew Carter and tell them the bad news. Especially if they were not implicated. "He took a deep breath" "Thank you for telling me, Inspector but I really don't know how I can help. As you know, I left before Josephine and nothing seemed amiss between the professor and his wife. In fact, I don't remember speaking to Mrs Carter and I only briefly spoke to Richard".

DI Wall held up a placatory hand. "It's alright Doctor Solace, I've not come to ask for information. I've come to ask a favour" curiouser and curiouser thought Solace. "Go on" he said warily after a brief pause. Wall took another long swig of his beer seemingly taking courage from it. " I've had a request to contact you from our police pathologist whom I believe you know. A Doctor Cyril Mills." Solace's heart sank as many had before him. Mills, or Dark, Satanic

Mills as one wag on the force had christened him, had a reputation as a brooding, saturnine man who could reduce a burly officer of the law to tears with an acerbic remark or withering look. Solace couldn't think of anyone he'd rather see less. "Oh Yes?" said Solace, barely disguising his lack of enthusiasm. Wall continued "Doctor Mills asked me to contact you because he knows you to be one of the best toxicologists in the country." "I can't believe Cyril said that." Cut in Solace "I've never known him say a good word about anyone. Besides I retired from active service over a year ago and he knows this. If He's not up to it, there are dozens of perfectly capable doctors from Addenbrookes and indeed elsewhere who can do his job for him." Solace felt anger rising up inside him. He knew he was being unreasonable and yet like a helpless on looker, unable to stop.

DI Wall placed a hand on his arm and spoke with a quiet firmness that stopped Solace in his tracks. Doctor Solace, I am well aware of Doctor Mills sunny disposition and I can understand your reticence. Nor can I force you to help him but I have certainly never seen the doctor in such an anxious state before. nor have I ever seen a body in a mortuary or anywhere else for that matter like the one they wheeled in this morning. Now, Doctor Mills freely admits this is beyond his field of expertise. He knows his request is highly irregular but he implores you to come to Addenbrookes and help him with his diagnosis". Solace looked into the Inspector's eyes and saw his own image gaze sheepishly back at him. He finished his whiskey in a single gulp. "very well" he said "but find someone to walk my dog".

Chapter 3

Momentum Mortuary

DI Wall called a junior PC who sullenly accepted the task of walking Spillsbury and about an hour later the pair approached the door of Rose Cottage. This was what the staff of Addenbrookes hospital delicately called its mortuary. A long, high room with a marble table at its centre and large metal drawers, a sink and workbench taking up the left-hand side. When he entered, Solace could see a figure on the table covered with a white sheet and Doctor Cyril Mills sitting well away from it by the door on the far side. As Solace got nearer, he could see Mills was suffering from shock. Gone was the russet complexion and condescending curl of the lip. Cyril Mills had a vague, far away expression and greyish tinge that bothered Solace. He tried some flippancy as an opening gambit. "I love what you've done with the place Cyril but I do Prefer the Eagle on a Sunday" Mills looked up and answered in a quiet, hesitant voice "I'm so sorry Mark but I simply didn't know what to do." Mills looked like he was about to burst into tears. "Inspector," Said Solace quickly "I know it's against the rules, but can you rustle up a hot sweet tea for our friend here and I'll have a large, very strong black coffee." DI Wall nodded somewhat relieved and set off in search of the canteen.

"How can I help?" said Solace softly. "Mark, believe me" began Mills passing him a pair of surgical gloves "If I had a clue how to solve this, this" he motioned towards the figure on the table "I would never have come to you, but in sixteen years as a pathologist I have never seen anything like it. I know your reputation as a toxicologist and the only conclusion I can arrive at is Mrs Carter's condition is some sort of toxic chemical reaction. To what, God alone knows, but it's the only explanation I can come up with." Solace moved towards the table putting on the gloves but Mills stopped him with an arm on his shoulder. "Mark" said Mills in a hushed tone "if you will allow me, I think you should do this in stages. Start with the torso, give me your diagnosis, then move on to the head." Solace bridled inwardly. This whole thing was getting more absurd by the minute. His Sunday was being ruined by a man he couldn't stand. Now he was being treated like a squeamish junior Doctor on his first day on the rounds. However, the expression on Mills face made him reach for the sheet and lift it to expose Diana Carter's torso and legs. There had to be some mistake. There had obviously been a mix up by the porters. Solace turned to Mills, keeping the anger out of his voice. "What you have here Doctor Mills, judging by the blue/green mottling and skin slippage on the right rib cage not to mention the slight fur under the left breast, is a cadaver left out at room temperature for about two and a half weeks. Do I win the holiday?" Mills looked grimly at the floor "I promise you. The decomposition rate of this body has increased far beyond the laws of medical science. For Christ's sake Solace, I sat here and watched it happen!" Mills was now shaking.

He was obviously undergoing some sort of nervous breakdown. Solace willed DI Wall to come back and rescue him from this nightmare. He moved towards the sheet covering the head and saw Mills flinch and avert his eyes. He slowly raised the sheet and stood motionless. His brain trying to assemble the image into some sort of rational order. Diana Carter appeared to be wearing a mask or rather half mask. Everything above the mouth belonged to the woman he bumped into in the quad all those months ago. Where the nose ended, the mouth stretched and protruded out into a long, wide rictus grin. Showing long, sharp teeth that seemed to be stained red at the tips. Solace froze in a limbo of confusion. Gradually he pulled himself together and studied the face more closely. Gingerly turning the woman's head to the left and right. He paused for what seemed an age, trying to think of every conceivable reason for the physical aberration he saw before him. "This can't be possible, " he muttered to himself. "There are instances of physical disfigurement caused by severe shock but nothing on this scale. Bones just can't grow at this rate". "Do you see what I mean about the possibility of a toxic reaction?" ventured Mills eagerly. "I do" replied Solace "in as much as It seems slightly less impossible than every other theory I can think of. Have you

checked the pupils for dilation?"
Solace lifted the dead woman's
eyelids and let out a gasp.

There they were staring back at him
blankly. Two large jet-black opals.
Rag dolls eyes. Cold and inhuman.
The eyes he saw staring down at him
from that third-floor window. Now he
remembered and understood why he
couldn't before. That was what was
wrong with the picture. His mind
couldn't face the horror of that image.
Just then the door swung open and
both men jumped. DI Wall entered
with two
steaming plastic cups fresh from the

canteen. "You look like you might need these gentlemen." Said Wall, placing the cups in the doctor's hands, careful to avert his eyes from the table. Both men gratefully drank the hot sweet liquid. Thankful for the moments respite. "I think we need a pow wow in The Rose Garden " said Solace in between sips.

The late afternoon sun bathed the trio in a soft pink wash as they sat finishing their drinks in the small rose garden next to the mortuary. Solace felt wrung out but at the same time oddly buoyant. Faced with a seemingly unsolvable problem he felt his mind whirring in a way it hadn't done for some considerable time. He looked at his co-conspirators. Even some of Mills' old colour was returning to his cheeks. But that could be the fresh air thought Solace. "Well gentlemen" he began "let us examine the facts shall we." Inspector Wall shrugged his large shoulders. "I have to say Doctor Solace this is utterly beyond me. The last case I had was a missing motor bike in Ely. I really don't know where to begin." "Let us start at the flat. After the party." Continued Solace "you said Mrs Carter had a seizure Inspector. What made you think that?" "Well, I didn't know what else to call it" Shrugged DI Wall defensively. "I suppose the state of the flat might have made me come up with the idea. Also" here the policeman took a breath "The condition of Professor Carter himself" Solace looked hard at DI Wall. It was Doctor Mills" turn to speak. "Professor Carter was almost unidentifiable when they brought him in. It was pretty self-evident Mrs Carter was responsible. Carter's blood was on her teeth. It appears she bit through the back of his neck". Solace shuddered involuntarily. The three men stared into space, lost in thought for a moment.

"Right," said Solace, slapping his

knees hard and standing up. "This won't get the baby bathed." Inspector Wall, I want you to go to the Carters flat first thing and round up every bottle of pills, potions, draughts and lotions you can get your hands on and bring them to the main reception at King's College science department at 10am sharp. Doctor Mills, I'd like a sample of blood, bone, skin tissue and brain. I'd like that delivered to the same place at the same time if you would." The two men stared at him nonplussed. "Come on gents, stir your stumps." Smiled Solace
"We must imitate the action of the tiger". He then turned on his heels and walked off with a decided spring in his step. Doctor Mills turned to DI

Wall; his familiar sour expression had returned and noticed the policeman. "He's bloody well enjoying this" he said grimly.

Chapter 4

Dead End

Solace was drowning again. The water filling his lungs, pounding in his ears. He broke the surface of the waves gasping for breath. Spiralling. Arms flailing, legs kicking wildly. He saw the upturned boat in the distance. The sun playing on the hull, blinding him for a second as he fought to stay afloat. His lungs painful against his chest as he gulped down much needed air. Then he realised where he was and started to scream. The scream woke both him and Spillsbury, asleep at the end of his bed. He hadn't had the dream for months and now it was back in glorious technicolour. He felt his sweat sodden pyjamas against his skin and flung back his duvet.

"It must be all this recent excitement" Thought Solace out loud as gazed forlornly at himself in the shaving mirror. How he had managed to sleep at all was beyond him. Given the extraordinary series of events that had overtaken him over the previous twenty-four hours. But sleep had come finally in the small hours and with it the dream. He had convinced himself that he'd turned a corner. That time was smoothing out the memories. He fought the urge to dwell on the last moments of his wife's tragically short time on earth as he made coffee and scrambled eggs in his kitchen. Concentrating on the mammoth task ahead of him he dressed quickly and, after glancing at his watch, decided he just had time to walk Spillsbury in the botanical gardens before heading off to Kings College main reception for nine thirty. There to meet with Harold Sharp, lab technician of some years standing at the college and a man of infinite integrity and knowledge. He had nursed Solace through his formative months as a Professor of Biochemistry at the university just after the war. Moreover, he could be relied upon to keep his mouth shut and that was essential given the sensitivity of today's operation thought Solace as he mounted the steps to the main reception. He knew Harold would be there before him. His eyes lit up when he saw the squat, slightly dishevelled figure seated by the reception desk flicking through a newspaper.

Solace had telephoned Harold Sharp after he picked up Spillsbury from the now thoroughly besotted PC and returned home. He explained to the lab technician that
He needed his expertise and assistance. Moreover, Solace needed

access to the laboratories and equipment. He wasn't on the staff anymore and would technically be trespassing without his help. He also impressed upon the bemused Sharp the need for utter secrecy and that he would explain everything when they met. Hoping this brief, ominous exchange would suffice he quickly hung up. Solace really wasn't looking forward to that conversation. Sharp, for all his worthy attributes, wasn't blessed with an overactive imagination. That, however, was exactly the subjective level headedness Solace required in an assistant for this bizarre task. Harold Sharp grasped his hand warmly "It's good to see you Doctor Solace. It's

been a while. You're looking well".
"Liar" thought Solace and said so.
The two men laughed briefly and
started walking towards the
laboratories on the lower ground
floor. "I must admit I was somewhat
surprised by your call last night,
Doctor," said Sharp. "I thought you'd
retired." "I had" returned Solace
descending the stairs. "I was dragged
back kicking and screaming by the
Gendarmes yesterday. It seems
Professor Carter and his wife were
involved in some sort of fatal
altercation in their flat early yesterday
morning and the idiot of a pathologist
can't come up with any theories. I'm
sorry to get you involved Harold but
this shouldn't take long".

They reached Sharp's cramped office at the end of the corridor, flanked on either side by the college's four, well equipped laboratories. "Come in Doctor" said Sharp with a smile "I'll stick the kettle on". The two men entered and Solace took a seat by the window overlooking the south quad. "Thanks" said Solace gratefully, gazing absently at the statue of Henry the sixth in the middle of the lawn by the side of the chapel. "What would you like me to assist you with?" said Sharp, passing Solace a steaming mug of tea. "I can't thank you enough for helping me today Harold" began Solace. "Some samples will be arriving from Addenbrookes at ten. I'd like you to cast an expert eye over them for any abnormalities". "What kind of abnormalities Doctor?" Sharp's voice had an edge. A wariness Solace could understand." Here comes the difficult bit" he thought. "I don't know Harold, That's the problem. There's a chemical signature within those samples that I'm unfamiliar with. Sorry, that's very vague but it's the only way I can think of describing it. If you are willing, we will be assuming the role of code breaker this morning." he said, averting his eyes back to the statue. He had dodged the question. The facts were too wild. Too grizzly and weird to set before such a man as Sharp. The two men sipped their tea in silence for a moment. Just after ten a young man appeared at the door with the packages from Doctor Mills. Solace studied them briefly and handed two over to Sharp. "Right, we will divvy up the work. You do the skin and bone. I'll do the blood and brain. I'll be in lab one, you can be in three. Let's meet at one o'clock in the canteen and I'll buy you lunch. Deal? "Sharp took the packages "Deal" smiled Sharp "but I warn you Doctor; it will cost you. I've missed breakfast".

One o'clock came and found the two men staring forlornly at each other across a table in the college canteen.

Solace took a bite of his cheese sandwich and tried to mentally consolidate the last three hours. They had each gone to their separate laboratories and Solace had begun to familiarise himself with the equipment. The Bunsen burners, retorts, microscopes, vacuum flasks, test tubes and slides were all exactly as he had left them over a year ago. He set to work preparing the blood and brain samples before gingerly placing a small fraction of each onto a slide. It was a feeling of nostalgia coupled with a darker, painful sensation of loss that ebbed and flowed through Solace as he bent over the microscope, prompted by the faint smell of bleach and old varnished wood. Mentally shrugging them off and focusing his mind he concentrated on the image under the lens.

He had started with the brain sample. It seemed to comprise of a section of the cortex and the basal ganglia which are responsible for thinking and voluntary movements, and coordinating them between multiple areas of the brain. "The plasticity of the subject's brain would indicate a considerable amount of recent activity" noted down Solace. "corresponding with severe trauma or even seizure". That would seem to back up the Inspector's theory but wouldn't solve the issue of Mrs Carter's facial anomalies. What Solace really wanted was an MRI scan of her brain. But he realised that would be akin to closing the stable door after the horse had bolted. Whatever he could glean from her brain sample now was too little to make a respectable diagnosis. Suffice it to say her brain had undergone a severe shock but whether that had triggered her transformation was yet to be discovered.

A dead end. He hoped he would have better luck with the blood sample, which he now placed under the microscope and adjusting its range peered down at the slide. A multitude of blood cells swam into view. Solace reached for his pen. "there seems to be traces of a substance, possibly silicone based, containing respiratory pigments conducive with someone with a very high metabolic rate. Also, almost three times as many red blood cells than are normally found in an average human." Even more confusingly, red blood cells don't have nuclei, a quirk from when mammals began to evolve from fish, Mrs Carters however did. The remaining normal red blood cells seemed to be mutating into the ones with a nucleus before Solace's eyes. It seemed a foreign body was infiltrating the cell wall and changing the genetic code. But why?

When he spoke of his findings to Harold Sharp, in between bites of his sandwich, he was met with a quizzical expression. "Well, it seems to me Doctor Solace that Old Congo Carter shouldn't have kept such a big dog" "I beg your pardon" replied Solace. "In my humble opinion" continued Sharp pushing his cottage pie to one side in disgust "From the results of my findings. You gave me samples from two different subjects." Solace knew damn well that he hadn't but let Sharp carry on. "The skin is from a middle-aged female. Who, by the looks of things, died around three weeks ago? The Bone is a shaving from a jaw and judging by the density and tensile strength, it belonged to something large, powerful and canine with unusually strong marsketery apparatus. That puts my wife in the frame!" Sharp let out a sharp, staccato laugh that made Solace smile. Sharp went on. "A mate of mine in the army kept a German Shepherd and it was as good as gold. He let it sleep in his bedroom. One night it had a nightmare. Tore his face right off. Did a lot of damage. You never know where you are with dogs." They sat quietly for a moment.

Solace couldn't tell Sharp that the jaw bone did in fact belong to the wife of a university professor rather than The

Hound of the Baskervilles. "Harold" Solace began "I'd like you to do one more thing for me. I would like you to get two rats. One live, one dead, ideally before it's treated with formaldehyde, and inject them both with 15cc of the blood" Sharp looked even more quizzical. "Why the dead one Doctor Solace?" "I want to know if the blood affects the rate of decomposition" he answered truthfully. I really need to take a closer look at those blood cells. There's something in there that I can't pick up on a lab microscope. I don't suppose there's any chance I can use the Electron Microscope in the basement, is there?" Sharp did a sharp intake of breath. "Well," he shrugged, "that's Professor Carlyles department and he guards that thing like the Crown jewels. It is his pride and joy ""Great" smiled Solace "I'll pay him a visit and use every last vestige of charm I have on him. In the meantime, can I leave you to get on with rounding up those rats?" Sharp looked down mournfully at his cottage pie. "Believe me Doctor Solace. If it's a choice between the rats and the cottage pie I'll take the rats!"

A scant fifty minutes later Solace stood with Professor Carlyle in the huge, isolated basement laboratory, staring in admiration at the large Electron microscope. Kept down there because of its sensitive magnetic fields and immense value, it was an impressive sight and Solace had wanted to use it since it arrived five years ago. He had endured the "this is not a toy" and "I wouldn't normally do this" lectures from Carlyle and was prepared to play the submissive role in this relationship all day, if it meant getting the information he needed. Fortunately, he and Professor Carlyle were old friends and he had enormous respect for the bluff Ulsterman. A professor of advanced physics at the college for well over thirty years and a celebrated genealogist, Solace thanked Harold Sharp inwardly and felt he had struck gold with this encounter. He had explained everything to Carlyle including the change in Diana Carter's physical appearance without going into too much detail, hoping Carlyle might have come across anything similar during his long and celebrated career. "Can't say that I have Mark" said Carlyle in his warm Northern Irish brogue" his weathered features wrinkling into a frown. "You know as well as I do that bone cannot grow at that rate. However, I think it's your right to explore the toxic reaction theory, Certainly in the absence of a more rational proposition. Anyhow, if anything can help solve your problem this great beast can". He ran his fingers along its metal surface with affection.

The Electron microscope uses a beam of electrons rather than rays of light so it can reveal the structure of far smaller objects than a conventional microscope. It is primarily used for investigating microorganisms, cells and minute bacteria. Professor Carlyle, with a well-practised hand, dropped a tiny amount of saline solution onto a slide then, using a dropping pipette, delicately squeezed a fraction of the blood over it before placing it under the large condenser lens. He adjusted the slide on its holder and looked into the viewing port as the concentrated electrons became partially absorbed by the blood. The objective lens under the sample magnified it and projected it onto the projector lens. That lens then projected the final magnified image onto a fluorescent screen which Carlyle studied at great length while Solace tried not to interrupt or fidget. This operation was proving to be almost unbearable when the professor suddenly looked up, rubbed his eyes and seemed to steady himself against the table. "Well," asked Solace with all the enthusiasm of an expectant father. Professor Carlyle swallowed slowly and stared levelly at Solace. "From what I can ascertain" he began quietly "what you have here are traces of Chirt". "Chirt?" Solace raised an eyebrow. "Yes" continued the professor "Gunflint Chert. Possibly dating back three thousand million years." Solace looked confused. "Are you saying professor, that what caused Mrs Carter's physical changes is some sort of ancient rock?" he tried to keep the derision from his voice but without success.

"No" replied Carlyle softly "the rock is the carrier. It's what's inside the rock that could be the cause. It seems to be unzipping the DNA and bonding with it. Some kind of primitive bacteria, possibly algae, that I've never come across before" He paused, gathering his thoughts before going on. "About ten years ago I was in The States. Some chaps at Harvard were trying to trace the earliest forms of life. They had got hold of some of this Gunflint Chert and instead of drilling down into it, as They had done since before Pontius was a pilot, they rather cleverly decided to slice it wafer thin and polish it to within an inch of its life. They then put it under one of these" he motioned to the Electron microscope. "What they found were single celled micro fossils. These have a faint resemblance to the ones I saw at Harvard, those were, of course long dead, these, however, are not." Solace stepped forward and, looking through the viewing port, he saw what seemed to be the smallest organisms in existence squirm and writhe in a way that didn't seem at all natural. They appeared to vibrate. Also they gave off the effect of being close and at a distance at the same time, giving them an odd three-dimensional quality that gave him a strange sense of disorientation. They twinkled with an oddly coloured glow that unnerved Solace.

A faint wave of nausea passed over him. "what on earth is it?" whispered Solace. The professor shrugged. "Who knows. Once in a while the earth throws up something ugly" he said quietly. Solace noticed the old man's hands trembling. "Where would Mrs Carter have come into contact with rock that old" he mused out loud. "is she a keen traveller?" helped the professor "I don't think so" replied Solace "I know she went to Switzerland recently "Carlyle shook his head vigorously "no no, you need somewhere hotter. Somewhere close to the equator like Africa." In the back of Solace's brain a light bulb went on. "Congo Carter" he said almost to himself. He met Carlyles quizzical glare. "That's how Harold Sharp described Richard Carter earlier. Sharp's been helping me today. He called him "Congo Carter" the professor chuckled slightly "Good

Man is Sharp if a bit of a plodder. Yes, poor old Carter's nickname was Congo Carter. I know one shouldn't speak ill of the dead and all that but…" Carlyle caught sight of the laboratory clock above Solace's head. "Good Grief, is that the time?" he gasped "I've a meeting in twenty minutes. Walk me back to my study and I'll show you the photograph."

Chapter 5

A Rat! Dead for a Ducat! - Hamlet Act3 scene 4

As they walked, Professor Carlyle regaled Solace with his memories of Richard Carter's time as a student at Cambridge "He was quite a live wire as I recall" chuckled the professor as they skirted the great chapel by the banks of the river Cam on their way back to his study. "He had gone over to the Congo River Basin with two other Students as part of a much-heralded field trip just before the last war. They were out there to find new flora and fauna that might possibly help the university gain funding for its medical research department. I think

Carter was a biology student, a chap called Ferber was studying Chemistry and the other, I can't think of his name, was training to be a doctor. Anyway, when they came back everyone made a big fuss of them and they became local celebrities. I remember Carter took to it more than the other two and was forever droning on about his time in The Dark Continent like he was Henry Stanley or something. I seem to recall there being some nonsense bandied around about them finding the elixir of life, probably put about by Carter himself. He had a big bust up with Ferber in the canteen over shooting his mouth off. Finished his degree with a respectable two one and disappeared off the radar. Probably saw some active service during the war. Only to re-emerge twenty years later or so, somewhat cowed, with a professorship at the very university where he'd bored everyone senseless twenty years earlier." Carlyle then went on to relate tales of recent internal politics and various trivial minor scandals with his customary salacious relish.

Solace noted his deliberate avoidance of any reference to the loss of his wife and was thankful for it. That would be set aside for another, more fitting occasion. A time Solace was not looking forward to but knew was inevitable. They had reached the professor's study. Carlyle pointed and opposite was a large heavily framed, yellowing black and white photograph of a group of men standing in front of a wooden hut with a backdrop of what looked like a tropical rainforest. On the far right was a young, confident Carter in a fedora shaking hands with a miserable looking older individual who appeared to be a clergyman. Next to him was a figure straight out of H Rider Haggard thought Solace. Tall, strikingly handsome. With an Arian quality about the features and an easy, relaxed smile. The look was topped off with a pith helmet. "That's Andreas Ferber." Said Carlyle "quite the matinee idol isn't he." "And next to him?" asked Solace, noticing a squat, nervous looking, round young man with freckles and already receding ginger hair, shaking hands with a friendly looking local man, in traditional native garb. "Oh Yes" exclaimed the professor "Now I remember! That's Hollis. Hugo Hollis. Funny little chap. Very nervy, but, by all accounts, all the makings of a brilliant doctor. The real joker in the pack. When they came back, he dropped out, to use the American parlance. Didn't complete his studies. Went to work in his father's bookshop just off the market square here. As far as I know he's still there."

Solace thanked Professor Carlyle for his invaluable help and told him he wouldn't take up any more of his time. The professor said he was sorry he couldn't have been of more use, mumbled some sympathetic platitudes about Solace's wife and was privately very thankful the episode had drawn to a close. Solace set off back to the lab with the hymn Rock of Ages running through his brain. As he started to descend the stairs to the lower ground floor of the main building, he heard the sound of running feet close behind him. He turned and saw Harold Sharp careering towards him red of face and short of breath. "Oh, Doctor Solace there you are" he gasped "I've been looking for you everywhere" "What's the matter Harold" said Solace concern etched on his face. He had never seen Sharp move so fast in his life. The technician appeared to have the stitch and was rubbing his rib cage in discomfort. "I did what you told me" he said almost defensively in between gulping down air. "Please, you've got to come with me right now Doctor." They set off at speed for the laboratory where Sharp had been conducting the tests. "I injected the rats with 15cc of your blood sample just like you said. About half an hour later I was doing some paperwork. Just sitting there like, and the live rat starts making these weird noises and shaking like it was having a fit or something. I've never seen anything like it. I mean the noises it was making Doctor Solace! Anyway, it gets worse and worse. Then it starts throwing itself against the bars of its cage, like it's trying to get out or something. I thought sod this for a game of soldiers and came looking for you."

They had reached the door of the laboratory. All was quiet within. Solace slowly opened the door and peered inside. The rat's cage was on the floor empty. The two men gingerly entered the room, their eyes scanning every corner for the errant rodent. "Look," Said Solace examining the cage, "it's bitten right through it." A sizable, jagged hole was visible. The bars twisted and prized apart. Suddenly there was a scuttling sound and a rustling of papers from the far corner of the room. Solace felt his stomach cartwheel and his hair stood up on the back of his neck. Silence. A deafening hiatus that clutched his insides as he felt panic rising. Then they heard the scuttling again. The rat appeared to be running along the length of the room. The lab benches were obscuring his view. There was a metallic bang and he realised the rat had come into contact with the bin at the other corner of the lab. Slowly Solace edged forward, stooping down to get a better view underneath the work bench. Just then something shot past him, up from the floor, whizzing by it clipped his right shoulder. The shock made Solace gasp and stagger back. The rat seemed to be a fair size and the blow sent Solace reeling. He lost his footing and stumbling backwards, caught his head on the edge of the parallel workbench. He lay dazed on the floor, his head throbbing and saw the rat fully for the first time. Solace thought it was making for the open door but it stopped, turned and then seemed to regard Solace for a moment. Its large, jet black eyes, soulless and shining wet under the strip lighting.

Suddenly it made a low metallic nose unlike anything Solace had ever heard before and reared up on its hind legs. At that moment Harold Sharp had spotted a metal step ladder propped up against the wall by his side. He grabbed it and flung it the length of the room towards the rat in order to distract it. It fell short and landed with a clang beside Solace. He grabbed it and threw it over himself just as the rat launched himself at him. It flew through space and landed on the ladder, scrabbling to find a purchase. Its claws struggling to hold the metal rungs, its snapping, razor sharp teeth and maw inches from his face. Solace could feel the power of the animal's hate as it searched to find a gap in the

ladder's rungs. Solace moved it and shook it with every ounce of strength he had left in his arms. But the rat held on. He felt dizziness pass over him in waves. As he was weakening the rodent seemed to be gaining strength and he was finding it progressively difficult to keep the ladder raised. The creature seemed hell bent on getting to his face. Suddenly everything happened at once. The ladder felt like it was knocked from his hands then a loud bang rent the air. Solace looked up to see the figure of Inspector Wall looming over him, a gun in one hand and a plastic carrier bag in the other. He
seemed to be looking past him. Solace

turned and saw Harold Sharp clutching the back wall as if his life depended on it. His eyes clamped shut. About three feet away from him the remains of the dead rat twitched, its blood slowly descending the wall in rivulets next to the terrified lab assistant.

Solace guessed the policeman had kicked the ladder out of his hands and rather expertly shot the rat as it hit the back wall. Inspector Wall helped him up and they moved towards the now still rodent, next to a slowly recovering Harold Sharp. Solace knelt down and inspected the animal, being careful not to touch it. "oh, my ears and whiskers" he said quietly to himself quoting the Mad Hatter. "What in God's name is that?" breathed the Inspector, peering over his shoulder anxiously. "It looked like a rat from the back". "it was" returned Solace "look at its eyes Inspector. Those aren't normal rodent eyes are they?" Wall looked in astonishment. "my God! It's got the same eyes as Mrs Carter." He gasped." Well, the same shape and colour certainly" returned Solace. "But not the same facial deformity." Sharp stared wildly at the two men. "Bloody hell. Do you mean to tell me that the bone sample you gave me belonged to Congo Carters missus?" Solace stood up.

"just so Harold." Solace turned to the policeman "Inspector, this is Harold Sharp. Harold, meet Inspector Wall." The two men nodded a greeting. "Harold works here and has been helping me this morning. Talking of which Harold, where's the other one? The dead one you injected, where did you put it?" Sharp motioned to the far side of the room still looking at the creature on the floor. "On the bench there, by the door". The three men turned to the bench. It was empty. Quickly the men hurried over to where the rat had been "this is crazy" Said Sharp, his voice rising. "I injected the bloody thing and put it here. I swear I did". "For God Sake Harold" Said Solace sharply "why didn't you put it in a cage?" "Why the hell would I put a dead rat in a bloody cage?" Cried Sharp defensively and rather reasonably thought D I Wall. "Alright gentlemen. Let's all keep calm and have a look round for it shall we?. It's got to be here somewhere." He said. Just then the sounds of a commotion came from the corridor outside. The men glanced quickly at each other before dashing out of the lab.

Following the shouts and noise of doors slamming, the trio pelted down the corridor and turned the corner to see a vision of students tumbling through classroom doors in an attempt to escape the thing that was slowly moving down the corridor towards a young Asian looking girl, frozen by fear and pressed ridged against the back wall. The large rat was now very much alive and at the sound of the men's approach stopped and turned to look at them. Everything paused briefly as the creature regarded them. Weighing up the threat they might pose. Then it started making staccato, metallic noises that set Walls teeth on edge. "Is it speaking to us?" he said in a hoarse whisper" Solace slowly nodded, not taking his eyes off the creature. "Sounds that way Inspector. Do you reckon you could hit it from here? That was pretty fancy shooting back in the lab." Wall felt the revolver in his hand. "I was a marksman in the Met a few years back but I lost my bottle." Wall grimaced at the memory. The rat was about twenty-five feet from the men and about fifteen from the girl. It suddenly started to shake and then did something that the men would remember for the rest of their lives. There was a series of sharp cracking sounds and its jaw began to stretch and broaden out. Its teeth growing and elongating in accordance with it. Wall felt his heart pound against his chest and his legs shake against the pleats of his trousers. Cold sweat broke out on his forehead. Solace spoke quietly and calmly "Then you had better find your bottle again quickly Inspector or that girl's in trouble."

She had started to sob quietly and that had caught the rat's attention. It started moving towards her again. The girl fainted dead away as the creature raised itself up and sprang forwards. As the girl hit the floor, Wall pumped a bullet into the rat while it was in mid-air just above her head. Muscle memory or an extraordinary focus brought on by a fight or flight mechanism in the human psyche? Wall often contemplated this afterwards but had no more idea than the next man. The creature landed on the floor a few feet from the girl who was slowly coming round. She let out a terrified scream as the injured rat started to edge painfully towards her still making its dreadful noises. Wall fired two more bullets into the creature as the men ran towards it. Sharp reached the girl first and dragged her away along the floor, then held her in his arms while she sobbed uncontrollably. Wall reached the rat then, stepping on its tail, finished the chamber. Solace caught up with him and surveyed the bloody mess that now almost covered the end of the corridor. "Why did it take so much to kill it?" Solace thought to himself, catching his breath. Sharp slowly helped the shaking student to her feet and, putting an arm around her, turned to Solace. "I'm taking her to the medical room" Sharp glowered at Solace and moved away. The accusation in his face hit Solace like a brick. He had brought this horror to the campus. This nightmare was all his fault. He looked at the floor "how was I to know this would happen?" he said quietly. Walls answer was plain "You weren't" he replied flatly and started to walk back to the laboratory "Cheer up" said the policeman "I've bought you a present.

Solace caught up with Wall's vigorous stride. "What are you doing carrying a gun anyway?" he asked "This is Cambridge not Chicago" "this isn't my gun" explained Wall blithely "I found it under Professor Carters bed when I was looking for Mrs Carters nick knacks. You know, the makeup and medicines you asked for. It's a service revolver. Standard army issue. Kept it in mint condition by the looks of it". It should have been a Mouser thought Solace but fortunately didn't say it. "Obviously looks like Carter was expecting trouble" he said instead as they reached the laboratory door. Once inside Wall picked up the plastic carrier bag, he had dropped on hearing the commotion and, placing it on a nearby bench, emptied its contents out. Solace then methodically went through the items; lip sticks, make up, shampoo, various beauty creams. The usual purchases of an affluent middle-aged woman.

Oddly, most of them were recently bought. He sighed. "There's nothing out of the ordinary here. Rather disappointingly, there's absolutely no sign that any of these things, either singularly or combined, could have contributed to Mrs Carter's transformation. "Hold on" said Wall fishing in his jacket pocket "I found this in the kitchen bin".

He produced a small, empty plastic pill bottle. Solace examined it, turning it over in his hands. It was of the type found in countless chemist shops the world over. He opened it and sniffed the inside. Then he noticed something. "Inspector, this has been washed out recently. The cotton batting inside the stopper is damp. Now, why would you wash out an empty bottle of pills?" He thought aloud "unless there was something toxic inside perhaps?" The Inspector reached for the bottle. "Or the person it belonged to didn't want anyone to know what was in it." Replied the policeman. "You have a naturally devious mind Inspector," smiled Solace. Then he noticed the emblem on the top of the bottle stopper. Two letters stood out, embossed in flowery gothic. F P. "Do you recognise this logo?" The policeman studied it briefly. "Yes," he answered "Ferber Pharmaceuticals. Big Swiss-German

Chemical company. Chap called Andreas Ferber has laboratories out near Cottenham. Squeaky clean. Makes sort of beatnik, herbal remedies. About as much use as a chocolate fireguard if you ask me but there must be a market for it." Solace smirked at the reference then he remembered the ageing photograph opposite professor Carlyle's study. Ferber was here at the university with Carter. In fact, he went to The Congo with him. Professor Carlyle had mentioned something about the particles of rock in Mrs Carter's bloodstream coming from that part of the world. It was a tenuous link but better than nothing.

"Inspector wall" said Solace "I think you need to find out what was in that bottle. If I were you, I'd interview Ferber. He might be able to shed some light on its contents." Wall thought for a moment then gave Solace his most charming smile "Doctor Solace, I can't thank you enough for all your help over this. You have gone above and beyond the call of duty. If I could ask you one more favour?" Solace eyed him suspiciously "yes"? he said slowly. "If I could organise an interview with Mr Ferber tomorrow would you come along?" Solace was about to raise an objection but the Inspector cut him off "If I interview him on my own, I wouldn't know if what he was telling me was the truth. It would be a complete waste of time. I have absolutely no knowledge of medicine. Herbal or conventional. It would only be an hour or so of your time and might mean a resolution to this business. Please Doctor." Solace studied the policeman for a moment, rubbing his throbbing temple. Taking his hand away he noticed a small amount of blood on his fingertips and realised he had cut his head on the side of the bench when he fell. "You should get your head looked at," said Wall helpfully. "your right there Inspector" returned Solace with a grim smile "for ever letting myself get involved in this nightmare."

Solace slowly mooched home as if in

a trance. A light, yet persistent rain had started covering the streets and the bright morning sunshine had given way to a brooding, pessimistic canopy. Stall holders had started thinking about packing up and stood chatting to each other waiting for the first one to start the ball rolling. The streets were changing character along with their colour and now had the usual late afternoon cast of people shopping after work for their dinner and gaggles of loud school children laughing and gossiping excitedly. Not that Solace noticed any of these developments. The morning's events playing out in his mind with extraordinary sharpness. A host of disconcerting memories attacked him and he felt them all like body blows to his gut. Sharp's face as he led the terrified student away. The rats reluctance to die. Its hideous transformation and the noises it made confounded Solace and the scientist in him felt a desperate urge to find the reason behind them. When he closed his eyes, he could see an imprint of those sinister microorganisms with their odd glow and vibration, giving him a strange feeling of excitement. Plus, the pain in his head had turned into a dull throbbing that seemed to beat time with his pulse.

He had staggered out of the university

leaving Wall to deal with the carnage and immediately set off to The Eagle for "A Leveller". Jack, known as The Silver Fox because of his thick light grey mane of hair, noticed the cut to his head as he passed him his double Red Breast. "You been in a fight Doctor?" he enquired in his usual wry manner. "I was attacked by a giant mutant rat if you must know." replied Solace, taking a large swig of the fiery amber liquid. "You want Rentokil" returned the landlord, moving off to serve another customer. "Why didn't I think of that?" replied Solace to himself ruefully. He stood at the bar for what seemed an age, lost in thought, looking for all the world like the victim of a mugging. Slowly

finishing his whiskey with a less than steady hand and steeling himself to abstain from another, he resolved to set off home. Inside Solace a war was raging between his ever-diminishing nervous energy and fatigue with the inevitable outcome insight. He arrived home and the key in the lock sent Spillsbury waddling down the hallway to greet his master. Solace felt the dog's comforting fur between his fingers but was too preoccupied to make his usual glib remarks. Instead, he slowly climbed the stairs to his bathroom to run a bath and dress his wound. Once there, he stared long and hard at the mark on his forehead in the shaving mirror, white to
the edge of his shirt, trying to force

back the slow invasion of panic rising within him. There could be no doubt. This wasn't a graze or a cut caused by a collision with a bench. The thin, slightly curved two-inch line above his right eye was a scratch from an animal's claw.

Chapter 6

FERBER

"Morning Doctor Solace. How's Your head?" called D I Wall from the driving seat of his dark blue Ford Consul. "Fine" deflected Solace climbing in the passenger seat, his scar now covered with Elastoplast. Overnight he had slowly developed the cold, nagging paranoia of the hypochondriac. He had contacted Wall after his bath
to tell him he had a change of heart and would be interested to hear what Andreas Ferber had to say. Professional curiosity and, after all, it would be churlish to refuse if he could be of assistance after such an

awful series of events. The policeman thanked him profusely and arranged to pick him up outside his house at nine thirty the next morning. This gesture was not from any altruistic standpoint. Solace now knew he had skin in the game. A personal investment born out of self-preservation. Perhaps even survival. It was essential to find out what was in that rat's system and although presently Solace didn't feel anything other than a dull pain conducive with a minor blow to the head, he couldn't be sure if this wouldn't be the precursor to something far more horrific. It was this fear of the unknown more than anything that rankled Solace.

"I've been doing some digging" began Wall, noticing Solace's silence as they drove out of the city and into the Cambridge countryside. "Ferber saw the Carters three weeks before the murder. They went on a skiing holiday to The Swiss Alps". "Yes, I know. Completely out of character. What do you know about Ferber?" asked Solace, pulling himself out of his blue funk and letting Wall do the talking while he did this. "There was a big profile on his dad in The Sunday Times a few years back. Emil Ferber made a fortune after the war selling paint stripper to the Germans. Apparently, he was one of the few companies allowed to trade with Germany after the war, possibly because of his Swiss connections. There was a lot of repainting going on in Germany after the war as you can imagine." Solace smiled grimly and nodded in agreement. After college Andreas Ferber went to work for his dad at their factory near Bern. We lose him during the war but he reemerges about twenty years ago back here where he opens laboratories near Cottenham. Seems he wanted to take the family firm in a new direction. From the less than glamorous world of industrial chemicals to the burgeoning market of pharmaceuticals. No wife or kids. Donates a lot to local charities. Spends most of his time growing his business by all accounts." Well, it seems to have paid off. People have got more money and are generally more health conscious I suppose, nowadays" chipped in Solace warming to the subject. "There's certainly enough of his products on the shelves" returned Wall "My daughter swears by all this snake oil he's peddling". "You had better keep your scepticism to yourself when we meet him." Cautioned Solace good humoredly "he might slip some deadly nightshade into your tea!" This ruffled Walls feathers slightly and silence descended again. It was Solace's turn to start the engine. He decided to do some digging of his own. "You said yesterday you were in The Metropolitan Police. That must have been a very different life from sleepy old Cambridge Inspector?" Solace had grown to like DI Wall and couldn't help but be impressed with his professionalism and dogged pursuit of results. There was also something vulnerable about Wall that intrigued him. "That's right. It's a long time ago though" smiled Wall, after a pause, hoping this deflection would serve as a book end and nip this line of inquiry in the bud. "Fair enough," said Solace, understanding, and the two men discussed mundane, domestic issues, as shy men do when they feel the weight of far heavier topics on their shoulders.

Eventually, to their private relief, a view of Ferber's laboratories appeared through the trees to their left. Solace had to admit it wasn't what he had expected. Given Ferbers background he had been on the lookout for grey, soulless, municipal outbuildings. Headington Hall flickered through the trees in the morning sunlight like an old reel of slowed down film. The large

Georgian manor house was flanked on either side by perfectly manicured rolling lawns, a well-kept rose garden and sizable pond, overhung with weeping willows. As they rolled up the drive the sound of laughter and youthful voices filled the air. Pockets of what looked like students played Frisbee, sat on rugs talking earnestly, played guitar or just working quietly crossed legged by the water's edge. There was a pervading sense of calm and positivity, possibly aided by the bright morning sunshine, which gave everything the strange feeling of a Hollywood musical. There was something about it all that jarred with Solace. The place had the atmosphere of a college campus or summer school rather than a business. Solace rather stuffily doubted that Boots the Chemist had kids strumming guitars and playing games outside its laboratories. As they approached the Hall, they saw a young blonde woman waving at them enthusiastically from the large double doors at the front of the building. "Hi there" piped the light silvery voice "I'm Tammy" The two men, collectively feeling about two hundred and fifty, tried to get out of the Inspector's car in the most agile way left open to them. "Beautiful Morning" continued Tammy with a smile bright as the sun. The two men subconsciously sucked their stomachs in and straightened up as they climbed the steps. "Andreas is waiting for you." Beamed Tammy. Her strawberry blonde hair, perfect white teeth set off by the freckles on her nose and bouncy southern American drawl gave her an evangelical, almost Quaker quality that slightly annoyed

Solace.

It was like being hit over the head with a bag of candy floss he thought as they followed the short, light yellow summer dress down the long corridor decked out with tasteful, beautifully drawn images of plants and flowers. There was a uniformity to the décor that was tasteful yet corporate at the same time. It lacked the personal touch thought Solace as Tammy enthusiastically chatted away, aided and abetted by Wall, who had a nice line in small talk, born of years dealing with the general public. Gently steering the conversation his way to gain information. She had studied botany here at Headington Hall as part of her PHD at Kingston University three years ago. She then stayed on as one of Andreas "Helpers". He didn't have PAs, she stated emphatically. "Although, that's what you are", thought Solace. A rich kid whom Ferber had got running around him for nothing. "They are students from different learning centres around the world. They all stay here for free and learn about the beauty and healing power of botanicals" she gushed in reply to Walls inquiry about the young people they had seen milling around the front of the property. "The students take sabbaticals and use the facilities here to enhance their knowledge of their chosen subjects. It's completely nonprofit making and Andreas uses the revenue from his parent company to finance the venture. Or adventure as he calls it" Tammy laughed winningly and Solace knew the brainwashing had been a success.

This girl was reciting chapter and verse he thought as they slowed down in front of a door at the end of the corridor. On the door was a large polished bronze plaque. It read Doctor Andreas Ferber, Chief Executive, Ferber Pharmaceuticals. Solace felt an oddly potent anger start to rise in his stomach." Doctor of what?" thought Solace. "Doctor of dandelions? Professor of peonies?" This whole setup was starting to have a decided whiff of the Barnum and Bailey about it. He resolved to keep a lid on his mood as he felt a sharp, fleeting pain across his temple. Fortunately, it passed as quickly as it came. Tammy knocked on the sturdy oak door and a light, friendly voice with a slight accent answered from within. "Come in if you're pretty!" Tammy raised her eyes to heaven and smilingly shook her head to signify to those present that this greeting was a regular occurrence but at the same time the remark was simply banter and nothing more. Her mime read "Men! Will they never grow up?" The two men smiled back to signify they understood the performance.

She opened the door and a tall, strikingly handsome man in his mid-fifties got up from behind a large polished mahogany desk looking slightly abashed. "These are the gentlemen you asked me to collect from the drive Andreas." Tammy was obviously besotted thought Solace as she held Ferber's eyes with her own. He wondered how many male "Helpers" Ferber had. Probably zero.

"Thank you very much Tammy. That's very kind of you. Forgive me gentleman. I was preoccupied. I use that phrase from force of habit" He laughed a warm, easy laugh and soft lines appeared round his light baby blue eyes. The good wrinkles that show you have a sense of humour noticed Solace. Ferber continued "It was a saying of my fathers and I suppose it stuck. I am always getting into trouble with the students for it. Please take a seat Gentlemen". He motioned to the chairs on the opposite side of the bench. "Well, you certainly have a lot of them," said Wall with a smile, taking him up on the offer. Ferber laughed again "Yes, the locals think I'm either the Pied Piper or a white slave trader". Now it was the visitors' turn to laugh politely. Giving Solace time to study Ferber more closely. He was barely different from the yellowing photograph opposite Carlyle's study. Not an ounce more around the chin or waste. The light blonde hair hadn't come from a bottle. Fashionably worn a little longer these days, it gave him the look of a much younger man. The immaculately cut tweed suit and salmon pink open necked shirt with wide collar was a stylish mixture of old and new. "This man could get away with murder" mused Solace. He had humorous self-deprecation down to a fine art and knew exactly the effect he had on the opposite sex as well as his own.

"Can I offer you some tea or coffee Gentleman?" continued Ferber "God

No! Sorry, I mean no thank you" blurted out Wall obviously remembering the Deadly Nightshade remark from Solace earlier on. "Nothing for me thank you" smiled Solace as he sat, enjoying Wall's embarrassment. Tammy was hovering in the background searching for an in on the conversation. "Andreas" she simpered "will you be coming to the Helpers supper this evening? It's my turn to cook." How Wonderful" replied Ferber beaming at the young woman until she started to melt. He turned to his visitors. "Tammy makes the best black bean stew you've tasted outside of the Catskills." Tammy changed to the colour of Ferbers shirt." However, I must bow out. I'm snowed under with work tonight. Forgive me Tammy. Please send my apologies to the others". She nodded with a defiant pout and turned on her heel. "Oh Tammy!" continued Ferber "could you please ask Marie-Anne to give Lab six a clean? Professor Ramirez needs it this afternoon." Tammy nodded with a smile and left the room with a toss of her long blonde locks and a complete lack of acknowledgement of the two men. This Made Solace feel ancient, invisible and out of condition compared to Dorian Grey behind the desk. Thank you for seeing us at such short notice Doctor Ferber." Began DI Wall. Ferber leaned forward, his face turning grave. "When you called me last night Inspector. I couldn't believe my ears." Ferber's voice was soft and hesitant. "I've known Richard Carter for over

thirty years. I was at his wedding to Diana. I attended Jo's christening. We were good friends. This is all so incredible…" Ferber's voice trailed away. He gazed into the distance for some time. Wall gently continued "I am very sorry to be the bearer of such awful news Doctor Ferber. I've brought Doctor Solace along with me today, as I mentioned in our call last night, because he is a noted toxicologist. He taught Biochemistry at Cambridge and also knew the Carters. We believe Diana Carter may have taken something which caused a major brain seizure and I need his help in identifying what that could be" Ferber nodded and smiled warmly at Solace. "I Have heard a great deal about you Doctor Solace. Your reputation precedes you. I hope I can be of service" Solace returned the warm smile.

"So, do I, Mr. Ferber" There was a slight wince. It was a small but accurate shot across the bows. An opening salvo and Solace could see it struck home. Ferber had chinks in his armour and he could see not being addressed as Doctor by a real doctor was one of them. Whatever charm school Wall had attended he was obviously their star pupil and he had cast himself as Good Cop from the get go. Which left only one role left to fill. Besides, all this politeness and status playing was beginning to get on Solaces nerves. He wanted to stir the pot a little. Ferber rode the punch and ignoring Solace turned to the policeman. "What makes you think I can help Inspector?" "We found an empty pill bottle with your logo on it at the Carters flat in London. I just wondered if you might be able to shed any light on its contents?" enquired Wall ". I am well aware you run a very successful business and supply a great deal of stores but, as you mentioned, you were a close friend of the Carters for many years. Do you happen to know what might have been inside that bottle? This is not, I hasten to add, an indication that we suspect you of anything Doctor, we are just in the process of ruling things out" Wall qualified. The easy, relaxed smile had returned. "I know exactly what was in that bottle Inspector. Ferber paused for effect. "Lavender, Lemon Verbena, Valerian and chamomile leaves. Diana Carter was plagued with cluster headaches after a recent accident. I made up a preparation to help dispel stress, promote calmness and sooth her headaches. A basic Anglo-Saxon

remedy dating back to the middle ages. Nothing that could have caused any trauma to the brain whatsoever." Ferber leaned back as though he had just played a full house and was trying not to rub it in. "Nothing from farther afield? "It was Solace's turn at the table. "I beg your pardon?" returned Ferber with a mildly quizzical expression that didn't interfere with his smile. "Nothing from the Congo River Basin for instance?" The smile froze and something akin to suspicion scudded across Ferber's countenance. Silence. "Sorry. I am not with you" he said slowly, regarding Solace in a new light. "You see Mr. Ferber" Solace was now raining down blows on his opponent. He
continued in a dry, slightly condescending tone. "I found minute

traces of silicone in Mrs. Carter's blood stream native to The Congo River Basin. Along with a bacterium I have yet to identify. But I expect to within the next day or so. Shouldn't be too difficult with all the means at my disposal. I know you travelled there with professor Carter while you were students. I just wondered if you could save us all a bit of time by telling us if you knew what it is?" Wall turned to look at him.

Solace was giving a terrific performance thought the Inspector. Knocking it out of the park. He was playing the bored professional having to take time from his important schedule to ask the amateur to tie up one or two loose ends for him.

Housed within that was the veiled accusation that Ferber was lying. All front of course he smiled to himself, but might shake Ferber up into revealing something. Solace however was privately surprised by his own brass neck and improvisational skills during this outburst. It felt like he was looking down on himself, egging himself on. Like he was two different people. "They say the onlooker sees most of the game" he thought. He felt somehow emboldened to continue in the role he was given. "Do you use any plants or flowers in your herbal remedies that come from The Congo Mr. Ferber?" That did it. "It's Doctor Ferber," said Ferber with an edge to his voice. The smile had changed to a sneer. "oh?" Solace returned mildly, "I'm so sorry. Where did you train?" he asked this with the sweetest smile he could muster. "it's an honorary title" returned Ferber defensively glaring back but keeping his voice polite and even. "And no. I do not use any plants or flowers, as you put it, from that part of the world. Although it does contain some of the most breathtaking flora and fauna known to man. Which is why I go there as often as my work allows. There are species in that region that I would dearly love to use and could potentially be of great benefit. But Sadly, officialdom coupled with the enormous expense makes it an unworkable proposition. I hope that answers your question." Ferber looked like he was wrapping up the interview. Wall felt compelled to rescue the situation. They were in serious danger of their quarry taking flight." Doctor Ferber" he began, smoothly changing the subject. "You said Mrs. Carter was prone to headaches after an accident. Would that have happened during the skiing trip you had with them about three weeks ago?" Ferber nodded somberly "that is right Inspector. I thought they needed a break so I invited them to our family chalet in Interlaken. "Were you with them when the accident took place Doctor" enquired Wall gently. Ferber nodded again. "Yes, I was Inspector. We had just finished a day's skiing and poor Diana slipped on the ice and cracked her skull" Solace thought for a moment then asked "How long did the air ambulance take to arrive?" Ferber shrugged defensively. "The snow was starting to come down pretty thick and getting worse all the time. It would have taken the air ambulance at least fifty minutes to get to us from

Bern. Once we had contacted them. We have a well-equipped medical unit at our factory less than half an hour away. We need to have. It's pretty out of the way up there and we employ quite a few people. Also, potentially toxic chemicals are routinely used in our work. As you can imagine. Anyway, it is far closer than Bern. In fact, we could see the factory from the slopes. I had to think fast gentlemen. I am not a medical doctor but I knew Diana was in a bad way. So, Richard and I carried her to my car. There then followed a very hairy drive through the slippery mountain roads. Visibility lessening all the time, but we arrived at the factory unscathed. We got Diana to the medical room and looked after her until the air ambulance arrived about an hour later."

A pause while the two men digested the information. It sounded convincing if a trifle rehearsed thought Solace. "You say" looked after" Doctor Ferber?" enquired Wall with a polite smile. "What did you do?" "Well," continued Ferber. as if struggling to recall the events. "As I remember it. I tried to compress the wound. Her head was badly cut open. So, I wrapped it tightly with bandages and packed ice around the skull. Then I used some pain killers. I forget which. Possibly simple ibuprofen to help bring the swelling down until the ambulance arrived. That's all I could think to do". "You didn't mind using ibuprofen then!" thought Solace but didn't say it. Instead, he thought he would pop down and join DI Wall in the charm department. "Well, that seemed to do the trick, Doctor Ferber.

Well done. I don't think I would have acted that quickly." He said with a warm smile. "Yes indeed" joined in Wall "You may well have saved Mrs. Carter's life." Ferber's modesty seemed genuine. "They are, I mean, were my good friends and I would have done anything to help them. Most people would have done the same. I feel sure." Wall was getting to his feet. "I won't take up anymore of your valuable time Doctor Ferber. Thank you so much for seeing us this morning. Your help has been invaluable." Ferber gave a short, self-deprecatory laugh. "You are very kind but I don't think It has Inspector. However, I wish you every success with your investigations. I'm sure the esteemed Doctor here will get to the bottom of it." Solace noticed the edge to Ferber's voice as he rose and the two men headed for the door. Ferber moved in front of them and opened it. "Oh, by the way" said Solace "do you happen to have any of those little pills handy you prescribed for Mrs. Carter?" Ferber beamed warmly at him. "I'm afraid not. They were a bespoke remedy made for Diana by me to the exact dosage. If she had asked for more, I would have made them, naturally, but I only made enough for that course of treatment". Solace nodded unconvinced and made to leave. Ferber stopped him at the door with an arm on his shoulder. "I understand your scepticism concerning my work Doctor Solace" he said with a wide grin. "I have faced it all my life. People are afraid of what they do not understand. But, let me tell you, there is more than one path to wellbeing. I have seen homoeopathy work first hand Doctor Solace. We are visited here by some of the leading experts in their fields. World renowned scientists, who all tell me our facilities are second to none. Discoveries are being made here all the time that convince me what we are doing will greatly benefit the human race." Solace looked blankly back at Ferber with a slight curl to his lip. "I wish you joy of it, sir. I really do." He said flatly. There was a moment between them. A squaring up that Solace felt was an acknowledgement of what they truly thought of each other. Then, Ferber broke the standoff with one of his professional grins. "You must come back and visit our laboratories. I would be delighted to show you round myself. I think you would enjoy it Doctor, and, who knows, I might even be able to convert you". He laughed. "Thank you. I'd like that." Solace's answer was polite yet noncommittal. "also" Ferber continued "I would be very intrigued to know your findings. It sounds like you are on the brink of cracking your case." Solace smiled knowingly. "Yes, Doctor Ferber. I believe I am. Good day to you."

A few moments later Ferber watched the Inspector's car disappear down the drive from his study window and swore sharply in German. The harsh, guttural oaths spat out of him like gunfire. He stopped dead and closed his eyes, breathing deeply for a few seconds. Then he moved to his desk and picked up the phone, quickly dialled a number. A voice answered at the other end ""Hans? It's Ferber. "He said softly "I will be returning very shortly. Prepare my father. Up the daily dosage to 20 ccs. Don't argue with me. Just do it! oh, and Hans, I shall be bringing a guest."

Chapter 7

Ashes to Ashes. - Church of England's Book of Common Prayer

Solace had always considered himself an even-tempered sort of cove. It was that focus, dry sense of humour and clarity of thought that had helped him with his work and latterly with dealing with the death of his wife. He meandered through life unruffled. Laid back was once used to describe him by a colleague and he had quite liked the description, though he would have preferred urbane. However, in the days that followed his moods had become gradually more extreme and erratic. He pitied poor Spillsbury. "It must be like living on a tropical island" he thought when he caught himself crying at a weather forecast on television while his dog looked on askance. Also, he had flashes of self-confidence and insight which bordered on the profound. Alongside these moments of euphoria, however, he had noticed himself becoming more and more scratchy and irritable, even prone to outbursts of anger at things he would normally consider merely mildly annoying. He put that down to the stultifying calm that had descended like a gloomy fog after all the excitement of the past days. Also, he considered his dark moods a reaction to his failure to solve the mystery of Mrs. Carter. He didn't want to consider, all be it momentarily, the darker implications. Even when the headaches grew worse.

When they had left Andreas Ferber's laboratories, he and Inspector Wall had concluded that while they didn't particularly like or trust him, they couldn't actually hang anything on Ferber. Wall rather dispiritedly resigned himself to ending his report with "Mrs. Carter died from a brain seizure, caused by brain damage resulting from a fall, or a toxic reaction caused by a substance or substances unknown." Cold, impersonal and inaccurate the policeman mused, but what else was there to say? Both men knew that summing up her transformation as an anomaly brought on by a simple allergic reaction or a fall was a lie but the truth was frustratingly out of reach and the facts themselves were stoically implausible. If he committed to print the events he had witnessed over the past two days he would be a laughing stock. He knew that. A certain kind of notoriety would follow him that he couldn't live with. A compromise would have to do and then he could go back to finding stolen motorbikes in Ely. A feeling of failure and anticlimax hung in the air between the two men as Wall shook Solace's hand after he had pulled up outside his house.

"Thanks again Doctor. you have been a terrific help through all this." he said trying to sound positive. Solace was rubbing his temple. The headaches had returned and, with it, a rising anger. He felt strongly that Ferber was involved in some way. He would have given his right arm to have found out what was really in that empty pill bottle. "I'm sorry I couldn't have been more help Inspector. But you have to admit it's been an eventful couple of days. We must do this again sometime" he said, trying to match Wall's light tone. The two men laughed and Solace hoped that he would see the policeman again. If only socially. He mumbled some remarks about keeping in touch and disappeared into his house before they had run out of things to say to each other. Three days later the invitation arrived.

Miss Josephine Elizabeth Carter
Is sad to announce the parting of
Professor Richard Gordon Carter
Ph.D. and Mrs. Diana Violet Carter
On Sunday the 22nd July 1966

A service is being held at
The East Chapel
Cambridge City Crematorium
On Saturday the 18th of August at
11am.

Please join us afterwards for a light lunch The Park Hotel

RSVP Miss Josephine Carter
(Address withheld)

Another invitation from the Carters he felt under qualified to accept thought Solace as he gazed dolefully down at the grey white card in his hand, sitting at a pew in the small but draughty chapel on that Saturday morning in mid-August. The service held few surprises. He had just finished singing Jerusalem. A hymn he particularly detested as it was his old school song and brought back memories of cold tapioca pudding, being constantly called Solids by the prefects and freezing cold afternoons on the playing fields. He glanced round and counted the heads again. Not even double figures. There was Leung and Smollet looking as bemused as he felt at being there. A cousin of Richard Carters and his large, bored looking wife who had come down from Edinburgh. Diana Carter's mother looking frail and ashen with what looked to be a female carer. Josephine Carter who had greeted him at the entrance with a tearful hug and what appeared to be sincere thanks for his attendance. She looked beautiful yet so fragile in her neat black dress, her short, bobbed hair catching the morning sun. Her eyes looked very tired like she had spent days crying. Solace felt painfully sorry for her and resolved to help her in any way he could in the future.

Two rows behind him sat the wolfish, leering presence of Andreas Ferber. In a sharp, expertly cut charcoal grey suit, matching tie and dark blue silk handkerchief to add that splash of colour. The service was basic to say the least. Solace wasn't expecting the funeral to be on the scale of Churchills the previous year but three hymns, a reading and the stock routine from the vicar, who seemed intent on avoiding eye contact with his congregation at all costs, about his father's house having many mansions felt like a sad finale for two human beings who had loved each other, raised a daughter, fought in a war and ended their time on earth so tragically. Still, thought Solace today wasn't about him. He mumbled through Abide with Me, considering it to be too unremittingly miserable even for a funeral hymn. Then on to the reading. Jo stood up and read 'Do Not Go Gentle Into That Good Night' by Dylan Thomas. Solace approved. He loved the poem and Jo did it justice. So much so that when she came to the final line, 'Rage, Rage Against The Dying Of The Light', it felt like she was addressing her father directly. There was a pleading in her eyes but also an accusation that seemed odd to him. Fortunately, there then followed the last hymn. 'How Great Thou Art'. Solace considered it a showstopper and always enjoyed singing it. When they all knelt in silent prayer at the end of the service to consider the passing of the Carters, he was overcome with a wave of emotion that almost engulfed him. It was not for The Carters that he wept but for his wife. Lost to him forever, somewhere in the depths of the Aegean Sea. They had tried so hard to find the body. Days turning to weeks. Despondency creeping through him like a cancer. A numb feeling of futility that tugged at his soul daily.

She was lost at sea. And now he was lost on land he thought bleakly.

Sharply Pushing these images away and covertly wiping his eyes, he focused on the Carters. The official line was Diana Carter had fatally injured her husband while having a psychotic episode during a massive brain seizure which eventually killed her. No wonder there was a poor turn out thought Solace grimly, rising from the pew and making to leave. He wouldn't go to the light lunch at The Park Hotel. He had marked the sense of unease and mild embarrassment from the few who had come today. The circumstances of their death wouldn't be easy to discuss over a plate of potted meat sandwiches. A hand touched his shoulder. It was Ferber. A mask of gentle sympathy on his handsome features. "Thank you so much for coming today Doctor Solace. I know Jo really appreciated it." Solace mumbled something about it being the least he could have done and turned to leave again. "I think we may have got off on the wrong foot at our last meeting Doctor" Ferber was being persistent and at his most charming. "I want you to know I hold you in the highest possible regard Doctor Solace" Solace made a noncommittal shrug with a smile to indicate his thanks. "my offer still stands" continued Ferber. "I would love you to come and see what we are doing at Headington Hall. I am convinced it is of great value to mankind." They were now at the chapel door and Solace could see an

end in sight. "I'll have a look at my diary" Solace gave the traditional, thinly veiled brush off and a slight sneer of recognition played across Ferber's lips. "Thank you," said Ferber tightly. "oh, by the way" he continued conspiratorially, as if the thought had just occurred to him. "how are you progressing with your investigations? Have you discovered what was in Poor Diana's system that might
have caused this tragedy?" This was what he was really after thought Solace. "I'm afraid I can't tell you that Doctor Ferber" Solace tried to keep his face solemn rather than annoyed. "The police have asked for that information to be classified. I'm sure you understand." Ferber looked mifted but fought bravely to hide it. "Of course," said Ferber with a curt

nod, sensing he could get nothing from him. "Goodbye Doctor Solace. I hope our paths will cross again soon." He turned and spoke to the vicar who was standing by the chapel door.

Once outside Solace made for Josephine Carter. He told her how beautiful he thought the service was. No, sadly he couldn't make the lunch as he had to take Spillsbury to the vets. No, it wasn't anything serious. Just old age. If there was anything he could do to help she must not hesitate to ask. While this conversation took place, Solace noticed two things. Firstly, how much Josephine resembled her mother and secondly that their conversation was being overlooked by a figure standing a short distance away, on the path leading up the hill to the crematorium gates. It was difficult to see because of the morning sun glittering through the trees behind the figure but gradually Solace recognised it to be that of Hugo Hollis. The third member of that Cambridge university expedition to The Congo. The image of that yellowing photograph flashed through his memory. Also, for a brief second, Solace thought there seemed to be someone with Hollis. a very tall, dark figure who looked to be standing at an odd angle. As his eyes focused on the scene, he realised it must have been a trick of the light. An effect caused by the positioning of the pine trees behind the man. Hollis was alone and still had the short round build. If a little heavier. There was even less wiry ginger hair and it was swept across his scalp in a vain attempt to cover a bald patch. Solace said his goodbyes to Jo and walked up the hill towards him.

At this the man turned and started to briskly walk off. "Mr Hollis!" called Solace after the receding figure. "Please wait! I need to talk to you. I was a friend of Richard Carters". Hollis stopped and turned to Solace, tears welling in his eyes. So, was I" he said softly, almost defensively. Solace held out a hand "I'm Mark Solace. I used to teach at the University alongside Richard." Hollis took the hand. "Well, Professor Solace, you seem to know who I am?" there was an edge of suspicion in the man's voice that Solace could

understand". "It's just plain Doctor I'm afraid Mr Hollis" smiled Solace "I never reached the lofty heights of professorship as Richard did. The fact is Mr Hollis, I'd really like to talk to you. You see, I was asked to assist in Diana Carter's most mortem and I found something in her system that I couldn't identify. It seemed to originate from
somewhere along The Congo River Basin. Solace stopped. A change had come over Hugo Hollis. Abject fear had spread across his face and he had begun to tremble slightly. There was a pause then his voice came out as a sad whisper. "She has taken the seed." There was an awkward pause. "would you mind if we sat down Doctor Solace? I feel rather unsteady on my feet" continued Hollis and the two men moved to a bench a little further

up the hill which appeared to be dedicated to the memory of a Mr Earnest Charles Bitnall. "I'm sorry if this is difficult Mr Hollis" began Solace after they had sat down and he saw that Hollis was gradually regaining his composure "I saw the photograph at the university. That's how I know you were part of the expedition. I just want to get to the bottom of this and set the record straight. For Richard's sake." He paused "Also, I will be honest with you Mr Hollis, I believe these bacteria, or whatever it is, has inadvertently entered my system and I need to find out what it is. Please help me".

Hollis laughed scornfully. "It wasn't

an expedition, Doctor Solace. Hillary went on expeditions. Shackleton went on expeditions. This was a publicity stunt by the University. A glorified field trip to drum up funding. Nothing more." He paused, gathering his thoughts then continued, bitterness in his voice. "I don't really like to think of those times but I'll help you for Richard's sake." Thank you. Mr Hollis" said Solace, gratefully. "we were nearing the end of our time out in The Congo" began Hollis reflectively "One day, both Ferber and I returned from another depressingly fruitless field trip up river to find Richard ranting hysterically about this kid who had miraculously been brought back from the dead by some local wise man, who had given him some strange seed. The lad had been dropped off by someone whom Richard took to be a relative as he was suffering from malaria. We used to get visits from the sick locals, you see, I was studying medicine and I didn't mind treating them if it was within my field of expertise. Anyway, I checked the boy over and he seemed ok. Ferber got very excited by this and wanted to go back to England straight away. So did Richard. I was behind with my thesis and said I would stay on a couple of days to wind things up at the mission. It seemed rude just to take off like that. They were talking about sorting papers out to bring the lad back so they could run some tests on him at the university. To monitor him in effect. You see. Anyway, I stayed on and they left the next day. Later that day the boy's dad came back for him. When our local helper

explained what had happened the chap didn't want anything to do with the boy. Totally went berserk. Like a bee in a bottle. Kept shouting and pointing up at the sky. When I asked the helper what the man was raving about, he said what he said didn't make any sense but I could tell it worried him. Anyway, I left a couple of days after that. And not a moment too soon. I couldn't wait to get shut of the place."
"Why?" asked Solace. Hollis turned to look at him, his face glistening with sweat. "The boy spooked me Doctor Solace." Solace couldn't help smiling inwardly at the school boy expression. "what do you mean "spooked" Mr Hollis?" He had the blackest eyes you've ever seen" said Hollis." He did nothing all day. Just sat on the porch looking out into the forest like

he was waiting for something. Anyway, I came back to Cambridge and a week later we discovered the Mission had been decimated. Destroyed. The two men in charge of the mission were killed. Completely torn apart. No sign of the child. The authorities said it was mountain gorillas but I'm not so sure. I never saw or heard a whiff of them for all the time we were there and anyway they are normally found far north of there." Anyway, when I got back to Cambridge, I suppose I had what you would call a mini nervous breakdown. I knew deep down I wasn't cut out to be a doctor and I went to work at my father's bookshop. I can't tell you how much that pleased him" Hollis smiled bitterly "I still kept in touch with Richard. We became good friends. He used to visit me at the bookshop. Said he liked the smell. Hollis laughed faintly and Solace smiled and nodded to show he shared Carter's appreciation of the faint, musty aroma of antiquarian books.

"I knew Richard was working with Ferber on something when we met up again after the war but he wouldn't tell me what. I think he was trying to protect me." Hollis laughed hollowly "he knew what a nervous wreck I was. The last time we
met he seemed very worried. He said he was concerned about the way things were going. I didn't know what he meant at the time." Hollis left the statement hanging in the air. Solace thought for a moment then said. "Mr Hollis, did you happen to see what

these seeds looked like?" Hollis nodded vigorously "Richard gave me a couple when we came back from the field trip. Ferber snatched the rest. He was like that. They look like a sort of metallic fruit seed or pip. You know, like a watermelon seed. Ferber has been trying to buy them off me for years but I'm not interested. They are my pension Doctor Solace. If He ever does find the elixir of life, I deserve a cut of the box office. "Would you mind if I took a look at one Mr Hollis? Said Solace. "I won't take it away from you. I can view it at your bookshop. I just want to see if I can match it up with anything we have on record at the university." Hollis laughed his hollow laugh. "Good luck with that Doctor, Ferber's been trying for twenty years and come up with nothing. But I don't see why not." He

fished in his pockets and pulled out a crumpled business card. "Come and see me at six o'clock tonight. It's just off the market in the alley at the side of The Arts Theatre." Thanks, I'll be there." Said Solace pocketing the card. He got
up from the bench then remembered something." Were you at the funeral today Mr Hollis? I don't remember seeing you."

Hollis looked at him flatly. "I wasn't invited, Doctor Solace." with that Hollis got up and walked towards the crematorium gates. Solace watched him go then turned to have one last look at the Carters final resting place. As he did so he noticed that two people had been watching his conversation with Hollis in rapt attention. They were Josephine Carter and Andreas Ferber.

Chapter 8

Death of a Salesman

For the rest of the day Solace was under the vague impression that he was being followed. Nothing definite. Just a feeling in the pit of his stomach and something just out of vision in the corner of his eye. He returned home, fed Spillsbury. Changed from his dark suit and fixed himself a light lunch of scrambled eggs. It was then that he was struck with such a blinding headache that he had to draw the curtains in his bedroom and rest on his bed with his eyes closed until it passed. This took a good hour and half. He then hauled himself to his feet and took Spillsbury for a long walk around the botanical gardens to clear his head. This operation had the desired effect. He then set off into town to pay a visit to Hugo Hollis.

The old bookshop was situated at the corner of a small but picturesque garden facing The Arts Theatre stage door. The peeling sign above the door read "Harold
Hollis And Son, Antiquated Book Dealers. Est 1921. As Solace approached, he saw the closed sign on the door. He tried it anyway and found it to be open. Stepping through the doorway he saw the bookshop comprised of two rooms. A largish shop at the front, its shelves bursting at the seams with browning copies of first additions and leather-bound

volumes of Wisden, Sherlock Holmes, Shakespeare and Dickens. Endless old ordnance survey maps covered the two small tables and haphazardly stacked on the floor there stood piles of old magazines such as Plays and Players and Film Review. Nothing very surprising here thought Solace breathing in the pleasant, familiar aromas. The far end of the shop led to a small anteroom. Probably meant for bookkeeping he surmised. The top half of its door was frosted glass which let out of dim glow from within. "Mr Hollis?" called Solace gently, moving towards the door. He rapt lightly on the wooden frame. No reply. "Mr Hollis?" he called again; this time slightly louder. Still no reply. He slowly opened the door and peered into the gloom. Hollis appeared to be sitting at a small wooden table, his back turned to the door, perched on a rickety looking old swivel chair. His head lolled back and Solace took him to be asleep. Probably the result of a large lunch thought Solace rather disingenuously. He called his name again and moved into the room. It was then he sensed something was wrong. Hollis was too still. He moved to the table and swung Hollis around in his chair.

Solace recoiled in shock. A deep gash stretched across the man's ample neck. Blood covered his torso and had seeped into his shirt. Hollis stared up at Solace in frozen terror with wide, glazed eyes. Flecks of blood covered his face and his mouth and chin were a deep red. Solace quickly surmised Hollis was attacked from behind then turned around as if to hide the fact. Poor Hollis, he thought sadly. So, terrified of life that he retreated from it only to die in such a barbaric and gruesome way. He hoped it was quick but grimly knew it wouldn't have been. Just then he heard a noise behind him and he quickly spun around. There stood Andreas Ferber in front of the now closed door brandishing what looked to be a small automatic pistol. His face a picture of grave sobriety. "Believe me Doctor Solace" began Ferber in a quiet, sombre tone. "If I could have avoided this I would have done. I repeatedly asked Hugo to give me the seeds and to keep his own council. I offered him a fortune. I wish I could have trusted him. I really do but I am too near attaining my goal to let anything stand in my way. The lives of the few must be sacrificed for the lives of the many" Solace knew now that whatever denotes insanity in an individual, Ferber was one of their number. Ferber wasn't ranting with a wild look in his eyes. He almost wished he was. Everything was expressed in a calm rational tone. That made it all the more unnerving. Solace was about to speak when he noticed a figure laying on a small battered settee against the wall at the far side of the room. The dim lighting had hidden it before.

It was Josephine Carter. A large bloodied kitchen knife lay next to her. As his eyes grew accustomed to the gloom, he could see that her face was creased into a mask of cruel malevolence. Pitch black eyes, like inkwells, gazed out at him with indifference. "Oh Jo" Solace whispered softly. "I see now. It wasn't Diana's face I saw at the window that night. Was it? It was yours. You spiked your mum's drinks and caused her to overdose". "You mustn't blame Jo" interjected Ferber, his voice sympathetic. "I asked her to. Her parents had become problematic." This last statement was expressed as if Ferber had been having difficulty with his car. "Richard had been progressively more frustrated by the course of our experiments. He had also taken a moral standpoint that closed his mind to what we could achieve. But I ask you, Doctor Solace, what is morally unjustifiable about saving lives?" It was clear Ferber was after understanding, even complicity for his crimes and Solace wasn't about to give it to him. "It depends on the cost." He said quietly, looking back at Hollis. Ferber carried on unabashed "I thought if I could show Richard how much I had achieved at my laboratory in Switzerland I could convince him to work with me on the final leg of my journey. Then fate stepped in and gave me an opportunity. In that medical unit at my father's factory Diana Carter died. She died, Doctor

Solace and I resurrected her."

"No prizes for guessing who Ferber thinks he is" thought Solace but didn't say it. "I gave Carter the choice" continued Ferber, his voice rising. "Did he want his wife to die or to live? Rightly, he chose the latter. Unfortunately, the formula was, at that point, unstable and Diana sadly experienced violent mood swings. Carter had a change of heart. He threatened to call the authorities. Close down the operation. After thirty years of hard work. Doctor Solace, imagine that!" Ferber's voice was now strident, defensive. "There was only one course of action left to take." Solace looked at Josephine Carter.

Her features were softening as he watched. The eyes returning to their natural shape and colour. She let out a soft, rapturous sigh that reminded him of the reveller in opium. "Get their daughter to kill them. For you." He said levelly. "don't like getting your lily-white hands dirty do you , Ferber." Ferber genuinely appeared to lose his composure for a moment. He could see
Ferber's finger tightening on the trigger. "she had the opportunity Solace". he said with a voice like bottled thunder. "she also volunteered willingly. Jo knows that we are at the precipice of a discovery that will alter the course of medical science." "Plus, you're pumping her full of these unknown bacteria to keep her

compliant. God knows what it's doing to her" said Solace, concern etched on his face.

"At a very mild dosage the user experiences great clarity and confidence. It acts rather like an opioid. I will wean her off it, in time" Ferber looked at her almost tenderly, then said as an afterthought. The facial distortion is disturbing, I grant you, but thankfully only momentary, side effect." He turned back to Solace. "besides" he said with a smile "aren't we rather straying from the point Doctor Solace? "his voice had regained some of its charm. "I believe what you came here for is over there." Ferber pointed with his gun towards the table next to Solace. He hadn't noticed before but there on the red lacquered table top were two small seeds. Solace picked one up and studied it under the light. "you have in your hand the gift of life, Doctor Solace." beamed Ferber evangelically. It did indeed look as Hugo Hollis had described it. A large watermelon seed, gun metal grey in colour. It seemed to shine under the light yet had a slightly rough texture as if it had been fashioned rather than grown. Ferber let him study it for a moment then continued. "it is my belief that the natives grind the rock down to a fine powder, add a little water, then form it into these capsules before baking them under the harsh African sun" Solace wanted to know more than anything how these natives stumbled upon this amazing discovery but kept his thoughts to himself. Instead, he said mildly. "fascinating. Any idea how it works?"

The Lazarus Seed" said Ferber imperiously "for so I have named it, bonds with DNA. As you probably know Doctor Solace, seventy percent of human DNA is what is referred to as Junk DNA. Its function remains a mystery to medical science. At the same time, within the human brain there are large dormant areas. Unused for no apparent reason. The Lazarus seed bonds with and then unzips the DNA. It then forms a link, a bridge if you will, between the junk DNA and the dormant neurons within the brain. Then comes the magic Doctor Solace." Ferber's eyes shone with passion. He paused for effect. "It ignites it! Switches on the light. The brain wakes up and the subject returns to life. Obviously, the beneficiary has to be given the seed pretty soon after life is extinguished, but I believe that, with work, the time frame can be improved. Especially with your help Doctor Solace."

Solace felt his stomach tighten. He knew the time to come clean was quickly approaching. Ferber, meanwhile, was looking visibly excited, his smile so broad it resembled the Cheshire cats, "with your recently attained knowledge of the seeds power we can finally arrive at my journeys end. You see, for years I have spent my life dedicated to replicating the seeds' chemical structure. After endless false starts and dead ends, I truly believe this has been achieved. The formula has been refined and the correct dosage mathematically calculated to within the smallest fraction. Will you help me with the concluding experiments? Just think what it means to be at the genesis of a new age of medical science. We really are at the brink!"

Solace tried to change the subject if only to buy him more time to think. "Is that why you had me followed today?" he said accusingly. "to lie in wait for me here and force me to help you against my will?" Ferber studied him quizzically for a second then laughed. "I think you may be suffering from some mild form of paranoia, Doctor. Please understand, If I had ordered you followed you would not have suspected it. I saw poor Hugo pass you his business card at The Crematorium and deduced you would be paying him a visit. I decided to get here first. A to collect the seeds and B to find out how much you actually know. Yes, old Hugo was very forthcoming. Amongst other things he told us you had arranged to see him at six o'clock. So, we decided to stick around, chatting over old times until you arrived." Solace was starting to panic. Ferber's obvious messiah complex coupled with the ever-present firearm was getting under his skin.

"Look Ferber," he stammered. "I'll come clean. All I know about this substance is that it seems to be a type of microorganism found in rock millions of years old. I don't know what it is because it isn't like anything else on record. I don't know why or how it does what it does. How it can even exist." The words were tumbling out of him now. "But you've got to listen to me, Ferber. You're dealing with forces you simply know nothing about. This thing exists outside of nature. It acts independently of all the natural laws.

I mean, Christ! Look what it does to people. To animals. You can't tell me that's natural. It's horrific! You have got to stop your experiments Ferber! Stop them before it's too late!" Solace fell silent. He realised he had been shouting. Ferber paused, regarding Solace with a mixture of pity and scorn. Then he spoke in a quiet, almost winsome tone. "A great pity. I had not expected such cowardice in the face of the unknown. Particularly as you are a doctor" Ferber pushed the last word out just enough to turn it into a weapon. "You will help me Solace" he continued slowly, "by either assisting me with my experiments or taking part in them." He glanced quickly at his watch. "But we are wasting time".

Ferber moved forwards and snatched the seed from Solace's hand and picked the other up from the table. "I'll take those I think, " he said, then swiftly moved to Josephine Carter. He checked her pulse then gently shook her awake with his right hand. While keeping the gun in his left firmly trained on Solace. "we have to move fast if we are to beat the weather". He said, helping the young woman to her feet.

"You really think you are going to get away with this?" said Solace defiantly nodding at Hollis." Yes, yes I do Doctor Solace" said Ferber simply. "If you look in Hugo's diary, his last entry is his meeting with you today. I believe that puts you front and centre in the forthcoming investigations." He turned to Josephine Carter. "We will dispose of the weapon on route" he said softly, placing the kitchen knife and her copper coloured backpack on the settee, then motioning Solace towards the door with his pistol he continued. "After you Doctor. There is someone I would like you to meet. And I know he's dying to meet you." Then cradling the weapon in the small of Solace's back added. With mock concern. "I do hope you're not afraid of flying."

Chapter 9

And Death Shall Have No Dominion - Dylan Thomas

The trio filed out into the darkening alley and crossed the road. Where a black Mercedes limousine was parked at the corner of the market square. A large burly man in chauffeur's uniform got out and silently opened the rear and front passenger doors. Solace sat in the back with Ferber. The pistol resting lightly against his ribs. They travelled in silence to a small private air strip a short distance from Ferber's laboratory. Throughout this journey Solace thought of many things but strangely at the forefront of his mind was one question. Who was going to look after his dog? He thought it was funny that the mind turned to trivial, domestic issues as some sort of defence against the more frightening realities. He considered raising the issue with Ferber but then dismissed it. Given the rising death toll he didn't think Ferber would make it his top priority. Probably a cat lover he mused darkly. They reached the airfield where a small but impressive private jet stood waiting. With the logo FP stencilled on the side. As they walked towards it Ferber said almost by way of an apology "Tax deductible. Doctor Solace. Also, we hire it out a great deal." Ferber seemed almost embarrassed by this show of ostentation." You must give me the phone number" countered Solace wryly. The pilot stepped from the cockpit to greet Ferber and they exchanged a brief conversation in German. Solace didn't have the gift of languages but worked out that the pilot was worried about the weather and Ferber was telling him there was no need but they had to get a move on.

Inside, the jet was less impressive. A cramped four-seater with miniscule windows. Ferber was politeness personified. Offering Solace some cold chicken from a hamper beneath his seat. Even a glass of chilled Gewurztraminer from Alsace. Solace graciously accepted as he didn't know when he would be eating again. Also, he was very partial to this distinctively herbal white wine. This ritual had a deeply civilising effect on the proceedings and the three made, for want of a better word, small talk for the two- and three-quarter hour journey. Ferber was turning out to be a humorous and attentive host and Solace was almost at the stage where he had forgotten this was, in fact, a kidnapping situation. Like all fully accredited psychopaths Ferber could switch characters as easily as changing his tie. Thought Solace. Suddenly Ferber leaned forwards and pointed at the window. "There she is!" he said with pride. Solace looked out of his window and saw Ferber's factory peeping through the clouds far beneath him. It was gigantic in size, dark and brooding with numerous outhouses nestled around it like ducklings around their mother. It reminded Solace of Battersea Power Station, but larger. Two enormous chimneys belched plumes of smoke into the night sky. They circled the edifice and came to land at another small landing strip at the rear of the factory just as the snow began to come down in large, thick flakes. "Made it!" said Ferber with a laugh, relief in his voice and motioned Solace politely towards the exit, once outside Ferber slapped the pilots back heartly and shook him warmly by the hand. A large Volkswagen jeep was waiting nearby and they hurried towards it. Solace realised he wasn't dressed for the occasion as he shivered under his tweed jacket. Josephine Carter walked by his side. She seemed at great pains to qualify Ferber's motives and indeed her own actions. "You must understand Mark" she said earnestly "that I loved my mother and father very much. But my father lacked courage right at the eleventh hour. It broke my heart to see him like that. If he had just seen it through to the end, he would have realised that there is nothing sinister or morally wrong about what Andreas is doing. Millions of lives will be saved. Men, women and children saved from premature and unnecessary deaths. Think of that Mark."

Solace turned to her and saw the fervour in her young eyes. "you're asking me to condone the murder of your parents Jo and that is something I can never do I'm afraid. Nothing will ever make that right. You know that. You must get off this terrible drug and get as far away from Ferber as possible" She looked up at him with emotion in her eyes and said softly. "Your wife Mark. She could be by your side now. Happy and healthy. You could be enjoying full, rich lives together". Solace cut her off sharply. "You leave my wife out of this!" he snapped and marched off ahead of her. These were the last words they spoke to each other.

They all jumped into the jeep. Ferber passed the back pack which contained the bloodied kitchen knife to the driver and they sped off downhill on a precariously slippery track towards a very large outbuilding furthest away from the factory itself. This unit was used to house a snow plough, two fork lift trucks and a snowcat. Also amongst their number were three quad bikes. Used around the outskirts of the factory to transport equipment quickly should the situation arise. The driver of the jeep, a tall, broad man in a great coat and fur hat, got out and pulled open the large metal double doors, fighting against their weight and the snow that was already beginning to bank up against the sides of the building. Once inside, Solace saw a decent sized shed had been built against the far wall. Probably to house cutting equipment and tools to maintain the vehicles in the outhouse he thought. As they approached it Ferber got out a set of keys and undid the heavy padlock on the thick oak door. As they entered Ferber switched on the lights and Solace could see that his earlier assumptions were far from correct. Ferber had converted the shed into a working laboratory which was split into two rooms. A smaller room, which was used as an observation post, with a door and large window running along the separating wall. Passed that there was the laboratory itself. They walked through the observation post and Ferber paused at the door of the laboratory. "Doctor

Solace. May I introduce my father?" he said with quiet pride. He turned the key and opened the laboratory door. Nothing could have prepared Solace for the image that greeted him.

The room contained a metal table on castors at one side and two sturdy metal chairs equal distance apart at the centre. There appeared to be thick leather restraining straps with tough metal buckles attached to both arms of each chair. Strapped into the chair on Solace's left sat, or rather slumped a very old, very frail looking man dressed in what looked to be a stained, dark orange factory boiler suit. Snow white hair hung in wisps around the sides of his head which lolled forwards. His pale, wrinkled skin hung down in jowls above a painfully thin body. As if it had been stretched like putty. It was difficult to tell if the figure was alive or dead, such was the scant amount of life force left in the frame. Ferber moved towards the figure and placed a hand tenderly on his shoulder. "My father is a very brave man Doctor Solace" began Ferber solemnly. "A great man. Towards the end of last year, he was diagnosed with a brain tumour. Inoperable. He knew the end was in sight. He also knew that my experiments were gathering momentum and I had successfully brought back from the dead several, albeit unsophisticated, life forms. Rats, dogs, but nothing on the scale of what I was aiming for. He then took the momentous decision to be the first human recipient of the Lazarus Seed. On January the 8th he died, Doctor Solace. I was with him when he passed. The apex of my life has been the privilege of bringing him back.

Since then, he has been kept alive on very low dosage while I laboured night and day to find the true formula. I now believe I have arrived at the end of my journey". Reaching into his pocket Ferber pulled out the automatic pistol and levelled it at Solace." You Herr Doctor will be the final guinea pig." Cold fear shot through Solace's body like a spike of ice. Ferber continued, motioning to the driver of the jeep, who grabbed the now struggling Solace and strapped him to the chair next to Emil Ferber before nodding subserviently to Ferber junior and departing "You see Doctor, it is all a matter of finding the correct formula" continued Ferber "refining it and calculating the exact dosage. Once that is achieved you cannot fail to have a successful result. First you will be injected with pentobarbital, a seizure medicine used for destroying animals. It has the same effect on humans. Don't worry it will be quite painless. You will just drift away. Exactly four minutes later The Lazarus Seed will be administered and you will be reborn as a new man. When we have found the experiment to have been a success, which I have every confidence we will, the formula will then be given to my father." Ferber gazed down at Solace triumphantly. Solace tried to keep the fear from his voice. "listen Ferber. You must know the seed can't be replicated. It's unlike anything else on the planet. And anyway, everyone's DNA is unique so each result will be different. You can't know the outcome of your formula until it happens and by then it will be too late. But the end result will always be the same. What happened to Diana Carter! You will keep propping up the user with higher and higher doses to keep them alive until it drives them over the edge. Each dose will be like Russian roulette" Ferber nodded to Josephine Carter who moved to the side table and started to prepare the syringe.

Solace decided desperately to try another tack. "Who will be the recipients of this magical formula anyway?" he said scornfully. Ferber looked back momentarily at the young woman. "Why, the great men and women of our time. Artists, thinkers, leaders in their fields. People with a gift to bring to humanity." Not sick children

then" Solace pitched this response to Josephine Carter who had finished at the table and was moving towards him, syringe in hand. "What about big business?" continued Solace. his voice rising. "Or politicians. I mean, just think of it, Ferber. You could have an army of fearless whirling dervishes that can't be killed. You could name your own price. There are governments out there who would bite your hand off. Don't tell me you haven't thought of that?" Josephine Carter's hand hovered over his arm and Solace detected a twinge of doubt travel across her face for the first time. Ferber's mouth twitched." I'm afraid the doctor is beginning to sound rather like your father Jo. Would you do the honours please? "With that Josephine Carter sunk the needle into Solace's forearm just below the elbow and emptied to contents of the syringe. Ferber leaned forward and whispered into Solace's ear. "See you on the other side, Doctor. Have a pleasant trip." Solace dug his nails into the padded arm of the chair, preparing himself for the thick blanket of tiredness that was about to press down on him. "Everything has its allotted span, Ferber. Things have to die so life can begin again "he reasoned."

Ferber smiled "Nature never dies. It is always changing and renewing. That is what you are doing, Doctor. The natural enemy of nature is stasis. As a scientist you must be aware of that ""You're insane Ferber!" he hissed through clenched teeth. "Who are you to decide who lives or dies? You're not God! "I am well aware of that fact, Doctor Solace". replied Ferber calmly "that weighty decision will be left to the experts. I have no desire to be involved in that difficult process. There will be panels of right-thinking individuals I imagine. I want no part of it. I am A political. Merely the supplier. Solace felt the room starting to go dark. He closed his eyes and felt the muscles in his face start to relax. Josephine Carter knelt down next to him and put her hand in his, "try to relax Mark" she whispered softly. "Just let it happen. You have to trust us. Let go Mark. Just let go. We will be here when you wake up." His breathing was getting shallow and everything was slowing down. "Please Jo." He whispered "Please help me. I don't want to die. Please. Tears were welling up in his eyes. He could hear Jo's voice cooing to him "It's all-right Mark. It will be alright.

Be at peace." She was treating this as some sort of spiritual journey thought Solace" Her voice seemed to be getting fainter, receding into the distance. Images were filling his mind as consciousness slipped away. DI Wall, Spillsbury, the rats, Hollis, even the vicar at the crematorium. Then for a second total blackness.

After which a figure came slowly into focus. It was his wife. She was smiling and holding out her arms as if welcoming him. He felt himself moving towards her. He had an intense sensation of happiness. He would be with her again. Everything would be alright. Suddenly her expression changed. She was shaking her head. She looked terrified and was raising her hands in front of her, as if for protection. She was receding again. Fading away. Then nothing. Absolutely nothing. This is impossible to describe or even comprehend. Because for the living there is, however small, always something. However, absolutely nothing happened to Doctor Mark Solace for precisely four minutes and forty-three seconds.

There was a flash of pain at the base of his skull and suddenly his eyes snapped open. He was back in the room. It was the same room and yet different. The colours were sharper, more vivid. He felt wonderful. New minted. Like he had slept for ten hours. Ferber and Jo were staring at him. big grins on their faces. They hugged each other and kissed briefly. Ferber said something but Solace didn't pick it up. He began to talk then realised he couldn't hear himself. Ferber crossed to him and checked his pulse, looked into his eyes, ears and mouth. He kept talking to him but Solace was getting nothing. He kept saying "I can't hear you" Ferber frowned and looked puzzled. He began talking to Jo who seemed to be disagreeing with him. Ferber kept pointing at his father then went through to the observation post and seemed to be writing something down out of Solace's view. Jo looked worried now but went to the table and picked up a syringe, moved to the prone figure of Emil Ferber who had been oblivious to all this excitement. She struggled to find a vein in his wizened, emaciated left arm but eventually did and gently poked the needle into it, emptying its contents. Then she returned to the table and started writing in a thick A4 notepad. Solace checked himself. He felt terrific. Completely normal apart from the hearing loss. In fact, better than he had felt in a long time. He couldn't remember anything after Jos comforting words of support. The trial appeared to be a success. Could it be that the ends did justify the means? Think what could be achieved in the field of medicine if the drug were to be used as a source for good, he thought. Suddenly there was a movement to the right of him. He saw Jo drop the pad and back away from the table.

He craned his neck and could see that old man Ferber was shaking like a leaf. Then suddenly his jaw stretched forwards and widened outwards. Rows of sharp, needle-like teeth grew from his mouth. Jos' screaming brought Solace's hearing back and got Ferber's attention in the observation post. Jo slowly backed towards the door and tried to open it but Ferber had locked it. Solace could see Ferber edging towards the outer door transfixed, as Jo screamed to be let out, hammering on the laboratory door for all she was worth. Next to him he could see old man Ferber's muscles writhing under his clothes like ships ropes and with a sharp movement he snapped first his left restraining bond then his right, as easily as if they were elastic bands. Emil Ferber slowly rose to his feet and then with unnatural speed shot towards Josephine Carter and buried his teeth in the back of her neck. With that, Andreas Ferber fled through the outer door and quickly snapped the padlock back in place and locked it.

Back in the laboratory Josephine Carter dropped to the floor and the thing that had been Emil Ferber stopped stock still for a moment. As if deciding what to do next. Then it slowly turned and regarded Solace, as if for the first time. If Solace thought he had known fear before that point he had been mistaken. Time froze as the creature slowly stalked towards him. Bringing its face close to his as if it were studying him. Solace got a whiff of something that reminded him of the lion house at the zoo as the creature impassively looked him up and down with cold, jet black opals. It kept turning its head from left to right as if confused. it didn't seem to know what to make of him. Then it raised its head and let out a harsh metallic shriek that turned Solace's blood cold. The Creature turned away and moved towards the door. It grabbed the door handle and in a single movement wrenched it from its hinges.

Meanwhile Ferber was pelting at full speed across the floor of the outhouse. He leapt onto a quad bike, turned the ignition key and pushed down hard on the kick starter. He revved the engine and the vehicle jerked into life. Thank God for Swiss efficiency he thought as he shot out between the large double doors and down the hill away from the factory. Although it was dark, the snow was coming down thick
and fast and the hill was steep and peppered with trees, Ferber's mind was sharp and he knew how to handle a quad bike. Plus, he knew the woods like the back of his hand, having spent

many happy hours playing there as a boy. Darting between the trees, hiding from The Boogg. A terrifying creature from Swiss folklore and the subject of the young Ferbers nightmares. He also recalled that the bottom of the hill linked up with the road that snaked down to the right from the factory. That road then joined the main road into Bern. He would head for there. Then he would contact Hans and work out what to do next. He couldn't understand why the experiment had failed. He had done everything right. Everything had been checked and rechecked adnauseum. Perhaps it had rejected the old formula that was still in his father's system. Pondering this, while at the same time negotiating the harsh terrain and worsening conditions, he glanced in his wing mirror. He saw a dark speck in the far distance moving at speed, zig zagging through the trees behind him. The quad bikes lights were picking out a flash of orange. It seemed to be making up the distance between them. He looked down at his fuel gauge. The dial was nudging red. For the first time in those woods for many years, he felt the icy hand of fear trace his spine. He picked up his speed and sharpened his concentration.

Back inside the laboratory all was not well with Solace. After the creature had gone, he had begun to feel shaky and his jaw had started to ache. Plus, the room seemed to be distorting. His eyes stung. He had tried calling out but his mouth felt like it was not his own. Panic overtook him and he started to scream with agony as his jaw felt like it was being pulled from its socket. Then a white-hot rage flooded his mind and he was filled with the bestial desire to kill, to destroy anything he saw. All life was his enemy and the only thing that would stop the pain was to cut it down. He saw that now, as clear as day. Total destruction would be the only solution to his ills. He felt a power and strength that he had never experienced before and it felt wonderful. He closed his eyes and the micro-organisms came into view. Then something happened. They were not writhing and squirming haphazardly as before but forming extraordinarily intricate patterns, like flocks of starlings. Swooping and wheeling to form shapes of such an unearthly and incredible nature that Solace marvelled at their complexity. There were stars and planets and what looked like constellations such as Orion's Belt and The Plough and others that Solace felt were unlike anything else in the universe. It filled him with wonder. It also seemed to be calming his rage. The shapes then seemed to move together to form a vertical line which filled out into the shape of a man. This image then started to fill his vision as if it were getting nearer. All of a sudden, he felt a presence in the room but, try as he might, his eyes wouldn't open. There was the sensation of a gentle pressure on the nape of his neck. As if it were being cradled by a large human hand. Manipulating it.

He felt incredibly peaceful and protected and heard sounds that resembled a form of low metallic speech in his right ear. Though he couldn't understand what the words meant, they felt comforting. Then all of a sudden everything stopped and a palpable stillness filled the room. He sat quietly trying to regulate his breathing and work out what was happening to him. Then from the depths of his stomach such a powerful feeling of nausea rose up in him like a tidal wide, that he vomited violently and repeatedly until mercifully, oblivion overtook him.

Chapter 10

At Death's Door

Bruno Borkhausen, security guard at Ferber Pharmaceuticals, crunched through the soft powdery snow and cursed his job. It was on days like these that he felt he really earned his money. He had watched the snow falling heavily all night while on his shift at the factory and knew it would be a nightmare getting home in the morning. Most of the workers stayed over on nights like these and were forever having parties that he had to break up on the orders of old man Ferber. This made him incredibly unpopular with the staff and he felt like a teacher on a school camp. The workers were allowed to sleep at the factory and there was even a large dormitory set up to accommodate them. Unfortunately, a sizable percentage of the workforce looked upon this as an opportunity to get drunk and capitalise on the situation by realising hitherto unfulfilled romantic trysts. Borkhausen knew that now instead of going home, having a hot bath and enjoying a plate of his wife's legendary Älplermagronen, he would be kicking his heels up here all day until the snow plough and snowcat were brought into action and the road from the factory was cleared. He had nearly completed his circuit of outbuildings and just had the largest and furthest away to check. The vehicle shed. He approached the large double doors and saw that they had been left open. "Sloppy" he thought. He would have to put that in his report.

He stepped inside the large hangar and saw everything was as normal. He was about to leave when something caught his eye. The door to the tool shed at the far side of the building appeared to be hanging off. As he moved towards it, he saw that this indeed was the case. The thick oak door was off its hinges and only still attached to one side of the frame by a sturdy metal chain and padlock. He supposed there were power tools, chain saws and even an oxy acetylene cutter in there that might be worth a few Francs. The thieves had picked a good night. No one around and the falling snow would have quickly covered their tyre tracks. He stepped through the doorway, carefully manoeuvring the door out of his way, and switched on the light. "Someone doesn't like doors" he thought oddly, when he saw the inner one had suffered the same fate. He noticed the shed had been converted into some kind of medical unit. There seemed to be red paint on the large window in the first room. Perhaps the existing sick bay wasn't big enough, he mused. Though it was an odd place to put it. He stepped through into the second room and stopped in his tracks. A woman lay on the floor to his right. It looked like her throat had been cut. Behind her there were two, what looked to be, dentist chairs. One unoccupied. On the other was seated a man. He was strapped to it and appeared to be dead. He was covered in vomit and had soiled himself. His head lolled forwards onto his chest. The cold air must have covered up the smell. Fighting back the urge to be sick himself Bruno Borkhausen ran from the room and reached for his walkie talkie.

In less than an hour and a half a police car and forensics van from Bahnhof as well as an ambulance from the Inselspital University Hospital in Freiburgstrasse had made it up the snowy factory road, thanks to the fast work of the snow plough and

Snowcat operators. Inspector Gabriel Meier of the Bern Kriminalpolizei, a bald, dry, methodical man in his forties looked across the carenage and sighed inwardly. The paramedics were stretchering the unconscious man into the ambulance before heading off as fast as they could safely drive back to the hospital in Bern. Meier had retrieved the man's wallet before they set off. His name was Mark Solace and he seemed to be a Doctor of some description, based in Cambridge, England. The girl had been murdered without question. Her head was just about connected to her body. The weapon used was a new one on him. perhaps specially made and based on some kind of saw. The forensics boys however had an even

more exotic version of events. A large blonde young man named Lucas pointed out that the jagged line around the girl's neck looked like teeth marks. The factory was quite remote and Meier knew that wolves and even bears were often seen on the mountains up from the factory. But they kept themselves to themselves and seldom if ever caused any trouble. No, this looked ritualistic. Perhaps even gang related. Crimes that did not frequently over burden the Bern Police, thought Meier. If the wild animal theory
were to be explored however, he mused, the animal could have been rabid, perhaps half starved. It broke in looking for food while some sort of bizarre experiment was underway and

killed the girl. Why then did he leave the man? Also, why was the man strapped to the chair and in such a state?

Looking round, the policeman discovered two sets of notes written with two different sets of handwriting, impossible to decipher and a table with two syringes and three empty vials on it. The unoccupied chair had two thick leather straps attached which were, rather be musingly, torn apart. On studying the doors, he deduced from the splintering of the frames that all previous guesswork had been wrong. Something hadn't broken in. Something had broken out. He didn't want to mount a search just yet because that always frightened the locals, the vast majority of which were a certain age and anyway he didn't know who or indeed what he was looking for yet. Also, thick snowfall was predicted for the next three days at least. One thing however, was certain. The man in the ambulance knew what had happened. He would question him when he was in a fit state. Also, he guessed with a sigh, he had to contact Interpol. Not relishing the mountain of paperwork about to come his way he said his goodbyes and trudged slowly out of the building and towards his car.

For two days Solace lay unconscious in a ward in the Inselspital University

Hospital, Bern while doctors and nurses around him fought to keep him alive. On the evening of day three he gradually regained consciousness and a dark, short haired nurse slowly fed him soup. On day four various doctors visited him and very gently tried to perform various cognitive tests. All of which he proceeded to fail dismally. On day five he had improved sufficiently to be carried out of bed and wheeled to the ward window while the nurses changed his sheets and washed him. This was the sight that greeted Inspector Meier when he came to interview him on that day.

Meier studied the frail, shrunken

figure gazing vacantly out of the hospital window. "Has he said anything?" he asked Doctor Steiner. A short bespectacled man in charge of his case. "Nothing," Steiner replied simply. "We've run various tests including CT and MRI scans "I don't think he knows who he is or where he is. He's lost the power of speech as well as the use of his legs and his cognitive
functions are very slow. When he came here his internal organs were all shutting down and there had been a recent tremendous surge of neural activity in his brain. If I didn't know better, I would say he had had a Hemorrhagic Stroke ""What's that?" asked Meier unenthusiastically "A bleed to the brain" answered Doctor

Steiner. "arguably the worst kind of stroke you can have. But there doesn't seem to be any evidence of the bleed. It's a mystery. I do know, however, that technically, he shouldn't be alive." Thank you Doctor." Said Meier, shaking the doctor's hand and trying to hide the disappointment in his voice. "let me know if he improves". On day six Solace was transferred to a private room, owing to the ward now having to be used for female patients only. It was muted that, thanks to his slow but steady improvement, he should be tried on solid foods.

That afternoon Staff Nurse Huber, a broad, jolly woman, whose grasp of the English language was not as good as she would have liked, knocked on the door of Solace's room, a tray of food in her other hand. She walked in briskly after receiving no reply and placed the tray on the bed in front of him. "This. For you" she said in broken English "solids". She noticed the patient's eyes flicker and a look of recognition crossed his face. As if he had just remembered something. However, the patient seemed to look cross. Maybe her pigeon English was at fault. She tucked him in and quickly left the room. Solace tried the cheese. It tasted tinny and metallic and the roll was too hard so he set them aside. He then turned his attention to the melon selection. He slowly raised the watermelon slice to his lips then studied it for a moment. Or more precisely the seeds embedded in the melons soft, dark pink flesh. He prized one out and looked at it for a very long time. Then Solace began to shout. Nurse Huber was alerted to the calls as she was just finishing her hot chocolate and rushed down the corridor. When she entered the room, Solace was sitting up in bed trying to talk. "Call The… police" his voice a hoarse, halting entreaty. "Inspector. Wall…. England…… Call… the……police. He then fell back on the bed unconscious.

Inspector Meier was duly contacted and he rushed to the hospital with Sargent Schneider in tow. Once there, they were ushered into the patient's room. Sargent Schneider sat at the back making notes while Meier positioned himself by the man's bed. Meier was the soul of patience, gently asking questions and slowly teasing out the information in between protracted rest periods, while nurse Huber looked in occasionally to check if the patient was getting too tired or to offer the

police officers, any tea or coffee. The interview lasted nearly two hours and was laborious in the extreme. Afterwards, the two officers thanked Solace and Staff Nurse Huber then walked out of the hospital and into the driving snow. They sat in their car for a moment in silence. Reflecting on the information they had just been given. Eventually it was Sargent Schneider who spoke first "poor man" he said softly. "Indeed" replied Meier, who was watching the windscreen wipers rhythmically push the snow from the car window almost as quickly as it was settling. "At best he is a fantasist" he continued sadly. "But I think it more likely his stroke has affected his brain." Schneider started the engine and the car pulled out of the hospital car park and into what passed for rush hour in Bern. The going was made slower by the unremitting snowfall. "Bloody weather" said Schneider after a while in an effort to make small talk. He didn't know Meier very well and felt slightly intimidated by the taciturn quality of his nature. "It's due to break tomorrow." Replied Meier" knowing a response was in order." Silence again. "At least we now know the dead girl's identity." Said Schneider, already willing the journey to end. "That's about all we learned today I'm afraid" replied Meier with a sigh, reaching for a cigarette from inside his great coat pocket.

Meier refused to believe Andreas Ferber was behind the murder. He had met him socially over the years at various police functions and liked him. He had a reputation as an affable, rakish playboy, albeit a little long in the tooth nowadays. A bit wayward in his youth perhaps but essentially harmless. The direct opposite of his saturnine, bullish father. Ferber was as far away from the Doctor Frankenstein figure that the man in the hospital had painted as it was possible to get. However, he would search him out and try to speak to him in due course, as a matter of procedure. He might even call out a search of the woods around the Ferber factory tomorrow if the snow lifted. After all, there was something out there even if it was only a wild bear. It needed to be killed. He had completely put out of his mind the splintering of the laboratory doors. "Are you going to contact this Inspector in England that he kept going on about?" Asked Schneider, lighting Meiers cigarette from the lighter on the dashboard. "Not if I can possibly help it" answered Meier sagely "you see Schneider, once you start getting other countries police forces involved you are in for a world of pain". Events happened the next day that put paid to all of Inspector Meiers plans.

Taking advantage of the break in the weather, young Willie Keller set out across the fields, stomping through the snow from his parent's farm house under a bright sunny sky, with his sledge tucked firmly under his arm, towards the hill beneath The Ferber Factory. The snow was thawing fast and turning into icy water that ran into the ditches that surrounded his father's fields. The hill was long and steep and he knew he could get a good head of steam up before he reached the bottom. Three hours later the boy returned home in a state of high excitement. Running into his mother who was coring apples in the kitchen, and claiming he had discovered a dinosaur. His mother, a practical woman, chided him for such high blown nonsense. Privately blaming his overactive imagination on the fact that he was an only child. Coupled with too much television before bedtime. The boy persisted in his claims to such an extent, however, that in order to mollify him she decided she would kill two birds with one stone by walking the dog and witnessing the great archeological find of the century for herself. Later that morning Mrs Keller made a rather shaky telephone call to the

Seepolizei Wohlensee police station in Schulstraße.

As afternoon arrived, so did three policemen and Mrs Keller took them to near the edge of the woods where the boy had first made his discovery. They found what they subsequently classified as a wild animal, lying twisted on the ground. It had been shot no less than six times. four bullets to the chest and two to the head. Fanning out, they also found a wrecked quad bike wrapped around a tree further down the hill towards the factory road. In a ditch right at the bottom of the hill they made their final discovery. Andreas Ferber. Dead, with a severe gash to the back of his neck. A report was made out and Inspector Meier was happy with its conclusions. A rabid wild animal had broken into a shed on The Ferber pharmaceutical Factory grounds. Killing an English woman named Josephine Carter then subsequently attacking and killing Andreas Ferber before eventually dying of gunshot wounds inflicted by Ferber himself. The animal's carcase had been destroyed due to the threat of a rabies infection. All wrapped up and nicely put away, the case was closed. What the report failed to mention was that the wild animal had been wearing a boiler suit. Also, forensics had discovered two things. That the saliva found on the young woman's neck was neither human nor animal.

Finally, and perhaps most bizarrely of all, the wild animal that Andreas Ferber had so diligently fired six bullets into had been dead for at least seven months.

Epilogue

There Are More Things In Heaven And Earth.. - Hamlet Act 1 Scene 5

Five weeks later, the eleven fifty-four Swissair flight from Bern to London Stansted touched down on time. Doctor Mark Solace slowly descended the steps of the aeroplane and crossed the tarmac under a bright autumn sun. Through his car window DI Wall could see how frail and thin his friend looked. Still, he had been expecting it. After he had talked to Inspector Meier, Solace had insisted on putting a call through to police headquarters in Cambridge. This was met with great excitement as Wall, when he eventually came on the line and was slowly brought up to speed on the facts by Solace, informed him that he was the lead suspect in a murder inquiry. Words Solace thought he would never hear. They had discovered Hugo Hollis sadly three days after his murder, seen his diary entry and set about finding the whereabouts of Solace. The police visited his home and, hearing his faithful old Saint Bernard howling in anguish, broke in. It was then that Wall decided to interview Ferber again, as he was one of the last people to see both Solace and Hollis. It transpired that not only Solace had vanished but Ferber also. He had just reached this frustrating impasse when he received the call from Solace.

After which, he immediately contacted a belligerent Swiss police Inspector who informed him that Josephine Carter had been killed and that they suspected a wild animal. It was all under control and there was no need for him to come out. Wall, sensing he was being stone walled, told his Swiss counterpart that Andreas Ferber was under investigation as an accessory to murder and that he strongly suspected he was in Bern. He asked the indifferent police officer to put out a search and arrest
him on sight. If he didn't, he would contact Interpol. This threat had the decided effect. The Swiss law enforcer said that the weather was bad at the moment but it was due to clear

in the morning. He would round up his men and mount a search. Wall strongly suspected the Swiss police were fobbing him off and clearly thought Solace had lost the plot. He set about trying to convince his superior to approve the necessary paperwork for him to fly out there. His superior dutifully reminded him that he had to be invited by The Swiss Police. He couldn't just invade the country "like Napoleon!" Not long after that he learned that the case had been closed. He asked for the case file to be sent over to him. If Solace was to be believed, it was the biggest piece of fiction since War and Peace. However, his hands were tied. It had been a matter for the Swiss Police. A notoriously insular and secretive body as Wall had found out to his cost.

Wall got out of his car and waved at Solace across the car park. Solace signified he had seen him and made for it. The pair shook hands warmly. "I'd like to say you look well Doctor Solace" began the Inspector, opening the front passenger door for him, "but it would be a pathetic lie." Solace laughed at the policeman's perennial candour. "You should have seen me six weeks ago," Solace said, slowly getting in the car. The Swiss are red hot on the old physiotherapy and put me through my paces. It was like a ruddy boot camp over there." Wall touched his forelock and attempted what he considered a chauffeur's posh drawl. "where to sir?" He asked differentially. "The Eagle" said Solace, a mischievous look in his eye. Wall did a double take. "You're joking!" he said. Solace looked sheepish. "just a small one Inspector. I deserve a treat after eating fondue for a month." Wall laughed "very good sir" he said and pulled out of the car park.

Fifty minutes later they were sitting at a table in Solace's usual spot in front of the unlit fireplace at The Eagle. Solace nursing a small Red Breast with lots of soda. The Inspector with his usual pint of bitter. "Thanks for sending my clothes. and for looking after Spillsbury" said Solace gratefully. "All part of the service," smiled Wall. "I left him in the loving arms of PC Harrison back at the station. He looked after him before. You'll have a job getting him back." Solace laughed and took a tentative sip of his whiskey. "sounds like you're lucky to be alive." Said Wall after a moment's reflection. Solace gazed into his glass. "I died out there Inspector." He said softly. "I could have turned into whatever that thing was that Emil Ferber became. But I was spared" Wall looked at him intrigued. "why do you think that was?" Solace thought for a moment. Divine intervention perhaps?" Wall's face was quizzical. Solace continued "I think the powers that be wanted all traces of the seed destroyed. That's why they took it out of my system. They nearly killed me in the process but it's definitely out," Wall looked concerned. "Are you sure about that?" he cautioned. "Listen," countered Solace gently. "I've had God knows how many blood tests over the past six weeks. They've found nothing. Plus, I would feel it. I think its prime directive was to make sure the seed remains a secret to everyone but a select few along the shores of The Belgian Congo. Killing me would have been superfluous to its plans." Who are these "powers that be exactly?" enquired Wall, wrestling internally with all this strange new information coming his way. I really don't know Inspector" answered Solace with a smile. "Perhaps it exists somewhere in the hinterland between science and magic?" This didn't really help Inspector Wall, who turned sullenly to his pint for comfort. "Solace smiled at the Inspector's confusion. "I must admit, I would have been sceptical myself a couple of months ago but now I'm not so sure. In the field of science there is a phenomenon called The Lazarus Taxon, which refers to organisms that reappear in the fossil record after a period of extinction. Or maybe it's an incredibly advanced, thinking microorganism if you're after a more fanciful scientific explanation but I'm sure it's much more than that." He paused regarding the Inspector's frustration.

"Regardless of the scientific angle, there are more things in heaven and earth Inspector than are dreamt of in your philosophy." Wall smiled. "You must be feeling better Doctor." You're back quoting The Bard. The friends laughed and sat in silence for a moment sipping their drinks. "You Know Doctor Solace " Began Wall after a while. His voice halting. "You asked me a while back about my time with The Met Police. I evaded the question. Well, I've been feeling bad about that." Solace was about to interject but Wall cut him off. "It's not much of a story I'm afraid. Especially after all you've been through, but, about ten years ago I was part of a stakeout watching a garage in Putney where a particularly nasty group of individuals were planning an armed robbery. They must have been tipped off and came out all guns blazing. A young girl got caught in the crossfire. She survived but something changed in me. I just couldn't do it anymore. I walked away." Solace leaned forward and said softly. "There's nothing wrong with walking away sometimes, Inspector. As long as you walk in the right direction." They sat together in silence for a moment.

Then Solace got to his feet. "Talking of which, I should wend my merry way. Let's keep in touch, shall we?" Wall looked surprised. "Where are you off to?" he asked, "to negotiate the safe handover of my dog from your PC." Answered Solace moving away. Wall laughed, following him to the pub door. "Let me know if you need back up." I will, "said Solace shaking the policeman's hand. Just then the landlord came out from the saloon bar. "Doctor Solace" he cried "it's been ages. Where have you been? I thought you were dead". Solace smiled at Wall covertly and said "I was. Sorry I've got to dash. Picking up Spillsbury." And with that he was gone. Wall watched him slowly walk up the street and out of sight through the pub window before turning back to the bar. "One for the road please Jack" he said, fishing some change out of its jacket pocket. "Is Doctor Solace alright?" said the landlord pouring Walls drink "he looks done in." "working too hard" evaded Wall, sorting out the right money on the bar. "thought so" returned the publican with a sniff. "I keep telling him he needs a holiday. Cheer himself up a bit. My sisters got a lovely holiday cottage in Cornwall. Very reasonable rates. Do him the world of good. But you know what he's like. He won't listen to me. You should try planting the seed in his head." Wall gave the landlord a long look and said "Do me a favour Jack. Don't mention seeds." He raised his glass to the aggrieved publican. Said "cheers" and returned to his seat by the fire to enjoy his pint.

Printed in Great Britain
by Amazon

49975870R00155